QUEER FACE

On the trail of a jewel robber, Superintendent John Brent from Scotland Yard lies in wait, with the police, outside a riverside country house — the thief's next anticipated target. But, avoiding arrest, the armed robber fatally shoots Brent and escapes onto his boat. When the launch is found, a single thumb-print is the only clue to the owner's identity. Brent's policeman son, vows to find the man responsible — the man he will come to know as 'Queer Face'.

GERALD VERNER

QUEER FACE

Complete and Unabridged

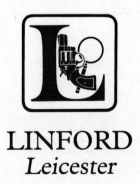

LINFORD
Leicester

First published in Great Britain

First Linford Edition
published 2012

British Library CIP Data

Verner, Gerald.
    Queer face. - - (Linford mystery library)
    1. Detective and mystery stories.
    2. Large type books.
    I. Title II. Series
    823.9'12–dc23

    ISBN 978–1–4448–1079–0

Published by
F. A. Thorpe (Publishing)
Anstey, Leicestershire

Set by Words & Graphics Ltd.
Anstey, Leicestershire
Printed and bound in Great Britain by
T. J. International Ltd., Padstow, Cornwall

This book is printed on acid-free paper

1

Behind the Wall

James Montgomery Brent had the distinction of being one of the few men attached to the Criminal Investigation Department of New Scotland Yard who had been admitted to that august body without serving a probationary period as a uniformed constable. In those days there were no colleges for the instruction of the embryo detective officer and entrance to the C.I.D. was obtainable only on merit. Jim owed his unusual distinction primarily to his father, for John Brent had been one of the Big Four and had held the rank of Superintendent at the time his tragic death had suddenly cut short his career.

Jimmy Brent had started as an office man, working under the melancholy Inspector Hallam who had been in charge of the fingerprint department, and it was a combination of luck and natural ability that brought him to the fore. It was he who had succeeded in finding Lew Sheldrake, bank robber and murderer, when nearly every detective in Scotland Yard had failed, and he did this working only in his spare time. He followed up this exploit by pulling in Mike Ellman, the 'Con' man, just as that enterprising gentleman was making a 'killing', and the wealthy American who had been saved from parting with seven thousand dollars was profuse in his thanks. They took Jim away from his filing cabinets after this and gave him the rank of sergeant.

For two years Jim continued to add minor triumphs to his record, working mostly under his father, and then came the tragedy that for a time darkened the brightness of his life, and left him with a savage desire to be revenged on the man who had been its cause.

There was a series of jewel robberies so cleverly carried out, so lacking in any indication of the perpetrator, that Scotland Yard was convinced that a new artist was at work. Usually the modus operandi will give the operator away, for crooks are creatures of habit and the professional burglar who makes an entrance by the pantry window will always effect an entrance that way, and would do so even if the kitchen window or the back door were wide open at the time.

There is a room at Scotland Yard filled with cabinets containing small cards, known as M.O. cards, and on these are tabulated the characteristics of all the known crooks, big and small. Here you will find particulars of men who always eat a meal on the premises they have robbed. Joe Brown's speciality is bread and cheese, Bill Smith invariably goes in for jam, others only make a habit of breaking into empty houses whilst the families are away, and so on. By consulting these cards after a robbery has been committed it is usually fairly easy to find one that tallies with the circumstances of the crime, and in nine cases out of ten the name of the man that appears on that particular card is the right one. But with these robberies the method was useless. There were no special characteristics and no clue was left behind.

In three months the unknown robber got away with an enormous quantity of jewellery — mostly diamonds — and neither he nor the stolen gems could be traced.

'It's my opinion,' said John Brent, who was in charge of the case, 'that we've got to deal with a new artist, and a new fence. This stuff is not going through any of the usual channels.'

The three men who sat round the big table in the conference room agreed with him.

'The question is,' said a grey-haired Chief Constable, 'how are we going to catch the fellow? That last job makes the seventh in three months, and we're no nearer to catching him than we were when we started.'

'He's a lone worker,' said old John slowly. 'He doesn't run with a gang, and that makes it all the more difficult to get a line on him. But I've got an idea; it may come off, and it may not, but it's worth trying. Have you noticed that these robberies have all occurred in the neighbourhood of the river?'

'Is that right?' The Chief Constable looked across at Jim who had been admitted to the conference and had brought with him all the documents connected with the case.

'Yes, that's right, sir,' he said nodding. 'The first was at Richmond, the second at Kingston, number three at Staines, the fourth and fifth at Windsor and Maidenhead, the sixth at Henley and the last at Marlow.'

'That's curious.' Chief-Inspector Mason, a dour man who spoke seldom, pursed his lips. 'What do you make of that, Brent?'

'He's working up the river,' answered the Superintendent, 'and I think he comes and goes by water. There have been several reports of a launch having been seen either just before or just after each robbery.'

'Well, what's your idea?' asked the Chief Constable a little impatiently. This was the second conference he had attended that day and he was a very tired man.

'This, sir,' John Brent leaned forward. 'Number eight is coming and I've got a hunch that it will be at Bourne End.'

Inspector Mason's still pursed lips emitted a whistle.

'The Rissac diamonds?' he said, and old John nodded.

'The diamonds are famous,' he said slowly, 'and the lawn of the house runs down to the river. It would be an easy job, and I think that's the place he'll go for next. If we keep a watch on the house we'll get him.'

They were in favour of his plan and it was adopted.

On a starless night, two weeks later, a silent-running launch drew in under the shade of the trees that grew over the river at the end of the Rissac's lawn and its solitary occupant made it fast.

As he stepped ashore he was surrounded by the patient men who had watched night after night for his arrival.

'I want you,' said old John Brent, and they were the last words he ever spoke, for with a snarl of rage the unknown robber snatched an automatic from his pocket and fired three shots at point blank range. Two of the bullets hit old John in the chest and he went down without a cry. The plain clothes men who were with him flung themselves on the murderer but he shot his way clear and made for his boat, leaving one dead man and three wounded behind him. They found the launch the next day. It was drifting down stream, but there was no sign of the man to whom it had belonged. Neither did they ever find him.

Jim had not been present on the night his father had been killed, and it was Chief-Inspector Mason who broke the news to him. He listened to what the older man had to tell him and the only outward sign of his grief was the whiteness of his face.

'Some day I'll find the man who did it,' he said calmly, but there was that in his voice that made Mason shiver.

There was one clue, and one clue only. On the polished handle of the gear-lever of the launch was found a single thumb print. The police theory was that the man had worn gloves but that the thumb of the right hand glove had split, for there were no other fingerprints of any kind. The clue was useless because it tallied with no other print in the record office, but Jim secured a photograph of it and carried it about with him in the hope that one day he would meet the man who had made it.

All this happened three years before he went on his eventful holiday, and during that time he had attained the rank of Inspector, and was earmarked for further promotion.

Dressed in an old pair of flannel trousers and a disreputable tweed jacket, his face burned nearly to the colour of mahogany, he was sitting in the shade of a tree eating a sandwich from the packet he had taken from his rucksack. He was spending his overdue holiday on a leisurely walking tour. Walking was a form of exercise that he loved, and he had planned to follow the winding course of the Thames into Gloucestershire, and if time permitted explore the lesser-known parts of Herefordshire. This was his fifth day and the weather was glorious even for the middle of June. He finished his sandwiches, took a long drink from his thermos flask, and lighting a cigarette leaned back against the gnarled oak at peace with the world.

The place where he had chosen to eat his lunch was a little copse of trees flanking a twisting lane and facing a high red brick wall partially covered with ivy that apparently enclosed the grounds of a big house, though nothing of this was visible. Outside this small oasis of shade the country lay shimmering in the heat of the summer afternoon. Jim began to feel drowsy. Scotland Yard and thief-catching belong to another world. This was a world of peace and contentment . . .

He awoke with a start as something struck him on the head and fell with a plop beside him. Screwing his neck round he saw a white object lying on the ground, two feet away. Reaching out he picked it up. It was a stone, around which had been wrapped a piece of paper. Wide-awake now, and rather curious, Jim unwrapped the paper and discovered some wavering lines of pencilled writing. With difficulty he deciphered the hasty scrawl:

'If anyone finds this will they inform the police that I am being held a prisoner at Dead Trees and in great danger.' The signature looked like 'Lesley Allerton', but Jim could not be certain of this for it had been so hurriedly written as to be almost unreadable. The message must have come from inside the high wall facing him. There was nowhere else it could have come from.

He read it through again. Was somebody playing a trick or was it genuine? He sat up and looked towards the wall, and as he did so he heard a sound that chilled his blood. From somewhere inside came a shrill scream, and it was the scream of a girl in mortal terror.

2

The Tenants of Dead Trees

That piercing scream broke off abruptly as though someone had hastily clapped a hand over the girl's mouth, and Jim's face set. The message was evidently not a hoax. There had been genuine terror in that cry so suddenly silenced. Something pretty serious was going on behind that high brick wall. Jim was on his feet now, and with the scrap of paper crushed in his hand he made his way quickly across the intervening strip of lane and looked up at the wall that towered above him.

It was a formidable obstacle. Nearly eight feet in height, the top was guarded by ugly looking pieces of glass embedded in cement. But for that he could have jumped, secured a hand hold and dragged himself up, as it was the barrier was practically unclimbable; certainly so without the aid of a ladder. He looked about him quickly. Somehow or other he was determined to see what lay on the other side, and presently he saw something which offered a possible means of doing so.

A few yards farther up the lane from where he was standing rose the trunk of a massive oak. It grew a good way away from the wall but one of its huge branches spanned the distance and projected a good three feet beyond the wall on the inside. Jim approached the tree with swift strides. The lowest branch was well out of his reach, but there were numerous excrescences on the ancient trunk and by the aid of these he succeeded in scrambling up until he reached the point from which the branches sprang. He paused for a moment astride the big limb he had selected as the best for his object, to recover his breath, and then began to work his way gingerly along toward the end. As he got farther from the trunk the branch bent alarmingly under his weight, but he went as far as he dared. He was now immediately over the broad, glass-protected coping of the wall and found that it enclosed the neglected grounds of a house.

Beyond a thick belt of shrubbery he could see across an unkempt lawn part of the weed-covered drive and the corner of a red brick building, the rest of which was obscured by trees. His eyes searched eagerly for any sight of the girl who had screamed but there was no sign of her. There was no sign of any living creature. The wilderness of the garden lay deserted in the heat of the summer afternoon.

He took a last quick look round without seeing anything more than he had done before, and edging his way back along the branch dropped into the lane. Brushing himself down he collected his rucksack from where he had left it beneath the tree, and flinging it across his back began to follow the wall with the intention of finding the entrance.

Presently he came upon it after almost making a circuit of the high wall. It was on the opposite side to the little lane — two heavy wooden gates, the same height as the brickwork in which they were set, the tops protected with a double row of crossed steel spikes. On each side of these, inside the wall, was a tree stump covered with thickly-growing ivy. Jim concluded rightly, that it was these two dead sentinels that had given the place its unusual name. He tried the gates and found that they were fast and immovable, but let into one was a small wicket containing a letterbox. This was also apparently locked for when he pressed the little flap it refused to open.

He had already settled on a vague plan and looked round for some means of making the inhabitants of the house aware of his presence. He found it in a small bell-push set in one of the brick pillars flanking the gates. Pressing the button he waited. He waited a long time. So long in fact that he had made up his mind to ring again when the flap of the letterbox in the wicket suddenly opened and he saw two eyes staring through at him.

'What do you want?' snarled a hoarse voice suspiciously.

'I'm sorry to trouble you,' said Jim, in his most engaging manner, 'but I wonder if you could oblige me with a glass of water . . . '

'No I can't!' snapped the owner of the unpleasant eyes, and the flap closed with a clink.

He moved away thoughtfully, following the road that ran past the gates. It dipped sharply, and in the valley he came upon the straggling outskirts of the village.

He had expected something of the sort, and consulting a signpost at the junction of a fork road he discovered that its name was Little Siltley. He took the branch road, and presently came upon the village proper. It consisted of a narrow High Street lined with cottages and small shops and at the end was what he had hoped to find — a new brick building with the blue lamp outside which testified that it was a police station. Jim entered the tiny charge room and the red-faced sergeant behind the desk raised his eyes sleepily from the newspaper he was studying.

'Yes, sir?' he asked in rather a bored voice.

Jim introduced himself and asked if he could see the Superintendent.

'He's in his office, sir.' The sergeant's boredom vanished when he heard the

15

rank of his visitor. He got down from his stool with remarkable agility considering his bulk and led the way to a door at the back.

After a preliminary tap he opened it and thrusting his head inside informed his superior that Jim wished to see him.

Superintendent Laker was a thin man, with high cheekbones and sparse grey hair. He looked at Jim over the top of a pair of steel spectacles as the flustered sergeant ushered him into the office.

'How do you do, Inspector,' he greeted in a surprisingly deep voice. 'What can I do for you?'

Jim took the chair he indicated and came to the point without preamble. The Superintendent listened to what he had to say without comment and frowningly examined the message that Jim gave him.

'There may be something in this,' he remarked when the Inspector had finished. 'I don't know much about the people at Dead Trees, a man and his wife have got the place, name of Hillbury, but I believe they're rather a funny lot.'

'How are they funny?' asked Jim, interested.

'Well, for one thing nobody's ever seen them,' answered Laker. 'The place used to be run as a private mental home, but it has been empty for years. Then these Hillburys took it eighteen months ago and have never gone beyond the gates since. They've got three servants, all men, and one or other of these do all the shopping that's necessary, but Mr. and Mrs. Hillbury never appear.'

'Sounds fishy to me,' remarked Jim, and the Superintendent nodded.

'I've thought it was queer for a long time,' he agreed, 'but of course I couldn't do anything. Shutting yourself up inside the wall of your own house isn't against the law. This, though, is a different matter.' He tapped the scrap of paper before him with a bony finger. 'It's my duty to inquire into this; between you and me, I'm rather glad of the chance.'

He rose to his feet, went over to the door, and called the sergeant.

'Tell Miller to get the car out,' he ordered, and came back to his desk. 'I'm going up to the house now,' he announced. 'Will you come with me?'

'Sure,' said Jim with alacrity, 'I want to meet these people whom nobody has ever seen.'

They chatted while they waited, and Jim discovered that despite his rather forbidding exterior Laker was a very pleasant man. Presently the sergeant announced that the car was ready, and Jim and his new acquaintance went out to it. A bucolic looking constable was standing beside the little machine.

'Will you want me, sir?' he asked, saluting as Laker got in.

The Superintendent paused for a moment.

'You may as well come along Miller,' he said. 'Get in the back.'

The constable obeyed, and with Jim sitting beside him Laker sent the car spinning up the road.

'Don't mention who I am,' said Jim as they got down outside the high wooden gates. 'Let them think I'm just an ordinary hiker.'

The Superintendent nodded, and going

over applied a finger to the bell-push. As before, there was a long wait before any notice was taken of his ring, then there was a click as the peephole letterbox was raised and the same pair of eyes peered out.

'What is it?' demanded the husky voice, and then as he caught sight of Jim: 'What, you 'ere again! Didn't I tell you — '

'Listen here,' said Laker in an authoritative voice. 'I'm Superintendent Laker, from Little Siltley, and I want to see Mr. Hillbury.'

There was a moment's silence from the man behind the wicket.

'I don't know if I can,' he began presently, and there was a note of apprehension in his voice.

'I'm afraid I must insist,' broke in the Superintendent. 'Will you tell Mr. Hillbury that I am here and that I should like a few words with him.'

'All right,' he said at last, ungraciously. 'I'll go and tell him.'

The flap snapped shut and they heard his shuffling footsteps receding.

'Nice, hospitable sort of place, isn't it?'

remarked Jim. 'I wonder what Mr. Hillbury will say when he gets my message?'

Whatever it was it certainly took him a considerable time, for nearly ten minutes elapsed before anything happened; then suddenly there came a rasping of a key and the wicket gate swung open,

A little, thin, wizened man appeared in the aperture and beckoned them.

'Mr. 'illbury will see yer,' he said, and his manner was less aggressive.

The thin little man with the unpleasant eyes surlily invited them to follow him and led the way up the path. As they rounded the bend, Jim got his first glimpse of the house.

It was a huge place, of red brick, softened here and there by patches of ivy. The upper windows were all protected by iron bars, which gave the place a forbidding and prison-like aspect. Wide stone steps led up to a pillared portico, and faced a circular expanse of tangled undergrowth, which had obviously once been a lawn. They crossed this and entered the house by the front door, which had evidently been left open for their arrival.

A man who was standing by the window, looking gloomily out, turned as they entered. He was enormously fat, but Jim realised as he looked at him that he had been fatter. The skin on the big white face hung in pouches below the eyes and at the corners of the small mouth. Several rows of wrinkled flesh bulged over his collar, and except for a faint reddish down he was almost completely bald. Jim thought he had never seen a more unpleasant-looking person.

'You wanted to see me?' he asked in a high falsetto voice, looking at Superintendent Laker.

Laker nodded.

'Yes, sir,' he answered, 'if you are Mr. Hillbury.'

The big face moved up and down.

'That's my name,' said the fat man. 'What did you wish to see me about?'

'Well, sir,' said Laker bluntly, 'I'm given to understand you are holding a lady here against her will.'

The almost hairless brows shot upwards.

'I don't understand you,' said Mr. Hillbury. 'What an extraordinary thing to say. What has put such an idea into your head?'

Laker briefly explained and produced the message. Mr. Hillbury read it, frowned, and clicked his teeth.

'Dear me, dear me, how tiresome,' he muttered. 'Of course I can explain this, Superintendent. My wife is subject at times to — well — er — shall we say fits of hysteria.'

Superintendent Laker stared at him.

'Do you mean that your wife threw that over the wall sir?' he demanded.

The fat man nodded and his expression was sorrowful.

'I'm afraid she did,' he replied. 'I'm very much afraid she did. She is subject to — er — hallucinations, and during one of these attacks she is under the impression that she is somebody else — in fact the — er — person who's signature is attached to this note.'

He sighed heavily. 'I have had a great deal of trouble before, that is why I have chosen this secluded place to live.'

Laker was obviously staggered.

'Do you mean, sir, that your wife is — er — is — ' He became incoherent searching for a word.

'Just a little unbalanced,' said Mr. Hillbury gently. 'Nothing really serious, but very trying. At such times she is under the impression that she is being kept a prisoner. The attacks do not last long and are quite infrequent, and at all other times she is perfectly normal.' He turned to the little wizened man who had remained standing by the open door, listening intently. 'Would you ask Mrs. Hillbury to come here for a moment, Dan?'

The man he addressed gave a swift nod and hurried away

'I've no doubt.' said the fat man, 'that she is quite recovered now, therefore I shall not mention the real object of your visit, but shall tell her that you have come to see me about some — er — local charity. I think that will be best.'

The silence was broken by the return of the little man this time accompanied by a tall woman whose age might have been anything between twenty-eight and forty. Her dark, sleek head was shapely and she moved with the swinging grace of a professional mannequin.

'Oh, Myra,' said Mr. Hillbury moving towards her, 'Superintendent Laker has called to ask if we will give a small donation towards the — er — er' — he floundered a little — 'er — police force. I have promised to send him a little cheque.'

The woman looked at Laker and bowed slightly, and then her eyes passed him and fixed themselves on Jim. They were large eyes, but just at the moment there was a vacant expression in their depths, which was easily accounted for if Mr. Hillbury had been speaking the truth. He caught a whiff of an exotic perfume as she moved over to a chair and sat down, and as he smelt the heavy scent his eyes narrowed. Superintendent Laker thanked the fat man and turned to take his leave.

'I'm sorry to have troubled you, sir,' he said, and Mr. Hillbury waved aside his apologies with a podgy hand.

'No trouble at all, Superintendent,' he

said suavely as he shepherded them to the door. 'Only too pleased to have been able to help.'

Glancing back as they came out into the wide hall, Jim saw that the woman was sitting motionless, staring fixedly at the open door, her hands loosely clasped in her lap.

'Is Mrs. Hillbury the only lady in the house?' he asked as they were going out, and the fat man shot him a suspicious glance.

'Yes,' he answered shortly, and Jim said no more.

They were conducted down the drive by the man called Dan, and when they, were back once more in the little police car and the wicket gate had been locked behind them, Superintendent Laker chuckled.

'Well, Mr. Brent,' he said. 'You struck a mare's nest, and I was a bit quick at jumping to conclusions. I'm sorry for that fellow. It's understandable now why they keep themselves to themselves.'

Jim said nothing; he was by no means satisfied. His sense of smell was very acute, and when he had first entered the big hall at Dead Trees he had noticed a faint perfume lingering in the air, and it was not the same perfume that was used so lavishly by Mrs. Hillbury.

3

Mr. Hillbury is Perturbed

The fat man watched them until they passed out of sight round the bend of the drive, and then he came back to the room where he had left the woman, mopping his moist face on a large handkerchief. She looked up as he entered and the vacant expression had left her large eyes.

'Have they gone?' she asked, and her voice was low and beautiful.

'Yes, thank Heaven,' he replied, a little shakily. 'Phew!' be breathed a sigh of relief. 'That was a nasty few minutes.'

He went over to the sideboard behind her, and she heard the chink of glass against glass.

'The policeman seemed to be satisfied,' she said without turning her head. 'I don't think you've got anything to worry about.'

'I'm not worrying about him.' He swallowed the stiff drink he had poured out at a gulp. 'It's the other man I'm scared of.'

'The other man?' she twisted round and faced him, her delicately pencilled brows raised in surprise.

'Yes.' He set down his empty glass and came over to the fireplace. 'Don't you know who he was?' She shook her head. 'Well, I'll tell you,' he went on. 'That was Detective-Inspector James Brent, one of the smartest 'busies' in Scotland Yard.'

'I — I thought he was just an ordinary holidaymaker,' she faltered. 'Are you sure — '

'Quite.' He mopped his face again. 'I recognised him at once, and it was a nasty shock, I can tell you.'

'Give me a cigarette,' she muttered, and when he had done so and it was alight: 'What do you think he was doing in the neighbourhood? Do you think it's got anything to do with us?'

The fat man shrugged his massive shoulders.

'I don't know,' he replied. 'I shouldn't think so. I don't see how he could have got on to anything. We're neither of us known to the police.'

He screwed up his small mouth and rubbed gently at his chin. 'More than likely his presence was just a coincidence.'

'Rather an unfortunate one,' she murmured. 'How did that girl manage to get away?'

'That was Clark's fault,' he answered. 'He was taking her round the garden for a breath of air when she slipped him. I'd no idea she'd managed to throw anything over the wall, and I'm sure Clark hadn't. She must have written that message and had it all ready, just waiting for an opportunity.'

'What made her scream?' asked the woman, deftly flicking the ash from her cigarette into an ashtray.

'Clark was annoyed and handled her a bit roughly getting her back to the house,' he replied. 'I'll take good care it doesn't happen again. We'll keep her locked up in future.'

A sudden thought struck her and she looked up.

'I suppose they won't attempt to search the house or anything like that,' she said, and apparently this had occurred to him also, for he said:

'They can search the house till they are black on the face — providing they've got a warrant — but they won't find anything.'

'What do you mean?' she asked, and he chuckled.

'You know the old well in the middle of the shrubbery?' he said meaningfully, and a startled look came into her eyes.

'You wouldn't — ' she began, and he interrupted her quickly.

'No, no. I don't mean anything like that,' he said. 'What do you take me for, a fool? But if there was any possibility of a search we could bind and gag the girl and lower her into the well at the end of a rope. She'd be safe enough there with the cover on, and they could search the house to their hearts' content.'

'I hope it won't be necessary,' said the woman.

'I hope so, too,' he agreed. 'But it's as well to have a plan in case of accidents.'

He looked round sharply as the door opened and the little wizened man came in.

'Well, they've gone,' he announced. 'That was a pretty cute idea of yours, guvnor, making out that she was dippy.' He jerked his head towards the woman in the chair. 'D'you think they swallowed it?'

'I'm hoping they did,' said the fat man softly. 'What have you done with the girl?'

'She's all right,' said the other with an unpleasant grin. 'Sam and George have taken her up to the padded room.'

'I'll see her,' said Mr. Hillbury, and brushing past the little man, went out into the hall.

Ascending the broad staircase heavily he presently found himself at the top of the house. Passing along a corridor he paused before a door at the end and rapped sharply with his knuckles.

The knocking sounded dead and without echo, and in response to his summons there came the grating of a key in the look and the door was pulled open.

A man who looked like a lower class prizefighter appeared on the threshold and stood aside as Mr. Hillbury entered. Another man, who was sitting at a small table in one corner, looked up from a greasy pack of cards he was shuffling

'Everything all right?' asked the fat man, and they both nodded.

'O.K., boss,' said the man who had opened the door 'You won't have any more trouble from 'er.'

'I should hope not,' said Mr. Hillbury gently. 'I should very much hope not.'

The room in which he stood was a strange apartment. From floor to ceiling the walls were padded with soft leather, and this extended even to the inside of the door. There was no window, the light being admitted by a skylight in the roof. The floor was composed of thick rubber blocks, and except for the table and two chairs there was no furniture. Lying in one corner was the figure of a girl, who was securely bound, and about her mouth had been tied an efficient gag, above which her eyes, wide with horror, stared up at the stout man. He advanced a few steps and stood looking down at her.

'You've caused a great deal of trouble, Miss Allerton,' he said pleasantly, but the high note held a note of menace. 'In future you will not be allowed outside the house. This is necessary to avoid a repetition of what occurred this afternoon.'

He bent forward suddenly and she shrank back.

'If you try any tricks again,' he snarled between his clenched teeth, 'I'll thrash you until you bleed.'

It was no idle threat, she knew that. This man with the mincing voice not only meant what he said but was capable of carrying it out — would rather enjoy it than otherwise. She watched him, her heart heavy with fear, while he talked with her two jailors about such mundane matters as supplying her with food and then as he went out she closed her eyes, fighting desperately to keep back the tears of despair that forced their way under the lids. Her attempt to secure help had failed, and not only failed but destroyed any possibility of her being able to try the same plan again.

Mr. Hillbury slowly descended the stairs and found Dan at the bottom smoking a cigarette.

'I want you,' he said. 'Are all the alarms working properly?' The little man nodded.

'Yes,' he answered. 'I mended the one the rabbit broke last night.'

'Who's on guard tonight?' said Mr. Hillbury.

'George,' answered Dan promptly.

'You'd better join him,' said the fat man, but at this the other muttered a protest.

''Ere, I was up last night,' he said. 'I want some sleep — '

'You can sleep from now till ten o'clock,' retorted Mr. Hillbury. 'That ought to be enough for you.'

The little man's face was sullen, but he refrained from argument.

'All right,' he muttered ungraciously, 'but what are you afraid of particularly tonight?'

He might as well have spoken to the empty air, for the fat man turned away without answering. The knowledge that Jim Brent was in the neighbourhood had upset him, but it was not for this he had ordered the double guard on Dead Trees that night.

He might be afraid of the police, but there was another whom he held in even greater fear, and it was because of this other he had come to live in the prison-like house. Because of him he had surrounded it with tripwires and electrical alarms, and engaged guards to watch night and day. If the police caught him it meant a long term of imprisonment, but that other — if he succeeded in getting in — meant certain death.

4

The Face in the Wood

Jim said nothing to Laker concerning his suspicions; that official was obviously satisfied, and apart from this Jim had decided to do a little investigating on his own.

On the way back to the little police station he casually announced his intention of staying the night at Little Siltley, and inquired if Laker could recommend an inn where he could put up. The Superintendent not only could, but did, and leaving him at the door of the police station Jim made his way to the Load of Hay, which, according to Laker, was the better of the two inns that Little Siltley boasted.

He had no intention of leaving things as they were. Mr. Hillbury's explanation of the message and the scream was plausible but he did not believe it. He was convinced that there was another woman in the house besides the one he had seen. To his mind the perfume was sufficient proof of this. A woman does not use two dissimilar scents at the same time, and that scent that he had smelt on first entering the hall was totally different from the rather heady perfume lavishly affected by Mrs. Hillbury. It was not much to go on but it was sufficient for Jim. Something crooked was going on in that unpleasant house, and he was determined to find out what it was. With this object in view he made up his mind to pay another visit to Dead Trees when darkness had fallen. It was going to be a surreptitious visit, unknown to the inhabitants of the place, and he was going to gain admission by means of the tree he had used earlier that afternoon.

He had no intention of taking the cheerful landlady into his confidence regarding his midnight excursion and there was no need for this. When he had examined his room he had noticed that the window overlooking the sloping roof of an outbuilding, which formed an easy means of egress and ingress without disturbing the landlady's careful locking up.

He waited until the place was quiet and sleeping and then started forth on his voyage of exploration.

The clock in the tower of Little Siltley church was striking twelve when he began to breast the slope that passed by the entrance to Dead Trees.

It was a beautiful night, warm and still. There was no moon, but the sky was clear and the stars hung in the deep blue like diamonds scattered in a velvet-lined bowl. He passed the heavy wooden gates and presently found himself under the spreading branches of the tree, which he had climbed that afternoon. It was very dark here. Beyond the oak tree was the edge of a thick wood, which grew close up to the walls of the house, and Jim was just preparing to climb the tree when he thought he heard a faint sound in the direction of this wood, and stopped to listen.

It might have been an animal of some sort that had caused that faint rustle which had attracted his attention, but on the other hand it might not. It was equally possible that it was someone from Dead Trees, and he had no wish to be discovered. Apart from the fact that he wished to be unsuspected by the Hillburys what he was going to do was strictly illegal.

If it came to the ears of his superiors at Scotland Yard he would be severely reprimanded. Not that this worried Jim so much as the fact that if he were discovered any chance of learning the secret concealed in that unpleasant house would be gone.

He pressed himself against the bulk of the big tree and listened intently, but now no sound broke the stillness of the night, not even a breath of wind disturbed the leaves overhead. He had almost persuaded himself that his imagination had been playing tricks with him when the soft rustle came again, this time accompanied by the sharp snapping of a twig. It was no animal that had made that sound, somebody was moving stealthily about in the wood. Jim slowly exhaled his pent-up breath. At that hour of the night it was hardly likely to be any ordinary person from the village. Whoever was there, concealed in the darkness, was either a tramp, or had some connection with the house, the grounds of which Jim was so desirous of exploring.

He became intensely curious to see more of this night prowler, and dropping down on his hands and knees he began to crawl cautiously towards the place where he had last seen the dim, red glow. He moved with infinite care making no sound and presently the spark of red showed again, nearer, barely a dozen yards ahead of him. The unknown was apparently standing still, at any rate he had not moved since he had last drawn at his cigarette. Jim crawled another yard or so, his progress necessarily slow, for the ground beneath him was rough and the faintest sound would give his presence away to the man he was stalking.

There was no sound now to guide him, and although he kept his eyes fixed on the patch of darkness where the little spot of red light had shone last there was no further sign of it. And then suddenly it came, close in front of him and seeming almost dazzling after the intense blackness. For one fleeting moment it lit up a hand and a face. It was the face that made Jim catch his breath and sent a cold shiver down his spine. White and featureless, it stood out against the dark background of the wood — an inhuman mask . . . puffy . . . shapeless . . . For one instant it was there and then it was gone.

5

Murder

Jim was so startled by the sight of that dreadful face that he momentarily forgot his caution. His full weight came down on a dead branch and it broke with a crack that was like a pistol shot in the silence. He heard a muttered exclamation and saw the cigarette strike the ground with a little shower of sparks; the swish of retreating footsteps rustling through the undergrowth came to him and he sprang to his feet. All further attempt at concealment was futile, and now that he had given his presence away he was determined if possible to get a closer view of the unknown man with the queer face, but in this he was to be disappointed.

For some time he followed the sound of the other's footsteps, penetrating deeper into the heart of the wood, and then suddenly the noise ceased altogether, and although he paused and listened intently he did not hear it again.

It was useless stumbling about in the dark on the off chance of picking up his quarry, and he decided to abandon the attempt. With some little difficulty, for he had rather lost his bearings, he made his way back to the oak tree. As he reached it, it occurred to him that it might be useful to secure the cigarette end the man had dropped. He could pretty well remember the spot and taking a box of matches from his pocket he lit one and began a search. At his second attempt he found it, and was glad that he had taken the trouble, for it was an expensive cigarette of an uncommon brand. He put it away in his pocket carefully and coming back to the oak tree began his preparations for getting into the grounds of Dead Trees.

It was less easy to climb the tree than it had been in daylight for the growths and protrusions on the trunk were not easily found. Twice his feet slithered from their precarious perch and he tumbled back on to the ground, but he managed it at last, and crawling along the branch that overhung the wall he dropped lightly on the other side. He landed waist deep in nettles and stood for a moment looking about him.

A yard away a wild tangle of shrubbery formed an effective screen and it completely prevented him from catching a glimpse of the house. He was rather anxious to see if there was a light in any of the windows, and he was moving cautiously forward to skirt the bushes when it suddenly struck him what a fool he had been. In concentrating on means of getting in he had completely forgotten to take any precaution for getting out. At the present moment if he were discovered, he would be caught like a rat in a trap.

The walls were unclimbable and circled the entire building. He paused and thought rapidly. Before doing anything else he must make some provision for a hasty exit, should the need arise. The question was, how? He cursed himself for not having thought of this before. It would have been so easy to have brought a rope and left it hanging from a branch of the tree by which he had gained admittance. However, it was too late to think about that now. Standing motionless in the darkness he racked his brains to think of a solution to this problem, and all at once one offered itself.

His eyes were getting accustomed to the gloom and he could see better, and at the end of the shrubbery he saw something that puzzled him at first but which he eventually made out to be a rustic arch. He went over to it and examined it closer. It appeared to be quite strong, and if he could only shift it, it was the very thing he needed. One side of it placed against the wall beneath the branch would form an effective ladder.

Stooping, he gripped one side firmly where it entered the ground, and tugged. He felt it give a little and redoubling his efforts presently succeeded in uprooting it. The other side was more difficult, but he managed this too. To separate one side from the arched portion was comparatively easy, and breathless but triumphant he carried the rough and ready ladder over to the wall and placed it in position. In case of emergency he was now assured of an easy getaway.

With that attended to, he began to seek for an opening in the shrubbery, and presently he found one. Forcing his way through, he came out on to what he concluded, from the different feel beneath his feet, had once been a path. There was no sign of it now, for it was choked with weed and overrun with brambles, but from here he could see the house.

It was in darkness, except for one light, which was burning in one of the ground floor windows. The curtains were not drawn, and there was no blind, and Jim decided that he wanted to see into the room. He moved cautiously forward but had scarcely gone two yards before his foot caught in something and he fell headlong. He was unhurt, but even as he scrambled to his feet he heard the faint jangle of a bell from the direction of the house, and instantly he guessed what had happened. He had fallen foul of a trip wire, which set an alarm in action. He had not been prepared for that, but the knowledge was very illuminating. Evidently Mr. Hillbury was scared of night visitors.

The alarm bell was still ringing and added to it came the sound of excited voices, and then the rattling of bolts being drawn.

Jim backed towards the shrubbery and crouched down in the cover of a bush. A door at the side of the house near the lighter window was flung open and in the dim light that came through he saw the figure of the little man who had let them in, standing on the threshold peering out. He was joined almost immediately by another taller figure and Jim saw that they both carried guns. The situation was decidedly unpleasant; he was unarmed and bare fists against a couple of big automatics would not put up much of a show. Added to this, if they started shooting they would have the law on their side. He was an unauthorised intruder and every man is entitled to protect his property.

He heard the hoarse voice of the man called Dan snap out some kind of an order and the next moment the darkness was dispelled by a brilliant light that flooded the neglected grounds; a pitiless glare that was as bright as the light of day. It came from a big floodlight fastened to the wall of the house and Jim's lips compressed into a tight line. If he attempted to move from his place of concealment now he would be seen. The only thing he could do was to remain where he was and trust to luck.

The two men came out into the brilliant glare peering suspiciously about them.

'There he is, over there!' The cry came suddenly from the second man and his companion swung round.

Jim thought he had been seen and was preparing to make a dash for his improvised ladder when to his surprise he saw that they were not looking in his direction at all, but towards the shrubbery beyond which lay the drive. The man called Dan raised his right arm and the pistol he held cracked viciously. Still firing, he ran forward and went plunging into the shrubbery. The other man stood for a moment undecidedly and then went after him.

The firing was still going on, but it was

fainter and farther away. Jim thought this was the moment to make his escape, and keeping himself well in the shadow of the shrubbery hurried as quickly as he could to the place where he had left the broken arch. Breathing a prayer that it would bear his weight he scrambled up and gripped the friendly branch above. He had scarcely got a hold when the old wood beneath his feet collapsed and he found himself swinging in mid-air. He succeeded in pulling himself up and a few minutes later found himself back in the lane, but the night's adventures were by no means over,

He was curious to know what was happening in the drive, and almost at a run he set off down the lane in the direction of the entrance gates. As he came within sight of them he slowed up. The wicket was open, but there was no one near it, and then he heard a rumbling step and a groan. He swung round towards a patch of trees at his right and as he did so a man came swaying towards him and almost fell into his arms. It was Dan, and in the faint starlight Jim saw that his face was ghastly white. He tried to hold him up, but he went sliding through his arms to the ground, and then he saw under the hand that was clutching at his throat the blood welling and with a startled exclamation dropped to his knees beside the prone figure. As he bent over him the man opened his eyes — and his lips parted.

'He did it,' he whispered. 'Queer Face!'

He tried to struggle up, uttered a long sigh and fell limply back, his eyes fixed and staring, and then it was Jim saw how he had met his death. Protruding from the side of his neck was a long knife.

6

The Thumbprint

The man was quite dead; it required no medical experience to know that. The surprising thing was that he had lived long enough with such a wound to be able to speak at all.

A hoarse shout broke in on his thoughts, and scrambling to his feet he turned in time to see the second man who had come out of the house with Dan running towards him, brandishing his automatic.

'Put up your hands,' he cried roughly, 'or I'll plug yer, see? I ain't standing no nonsense — '

'Put that thing away and don't be a fool!' snapped Jim angrily. 'I'm a police officer.'

'Police officer,' muttered the other, a little staggered, but making no effort to lower the muzzle of his pistol. 'You don't look like no policeman to me. I — '

He broke off abruptly and his jaw dropped as he saw the still form of his late companion lying at Jim's feet.

'What's 'appened to Dan?' he whispered huskily, and there was fear in his voice. 'What's 'appened to 'im?'

'He's been murdered,' said Jim shortly, and then before the other could reply: 'Is there a telephone in the house?'

The frightened man licked his lips and nodded.

'Then go and ring up the police station at Little Siltley,' ordered Jim. 'And ask Superintendent Laker to come here at once. Tell him what has happened, and say that Inspector Brent is here and told you to phone.'

The fear died out of the man's small eyes, and suspicion took its place.

'That's all very well,' he began sullenly, 'but 'ow am I to know that it ain't a gag?'

'Do as the Inspector says,' broke in a high-pitched, shaky voice. 'Do as he says, Cusher.'

Jim turned quickly towards the open wicket gate and saw the hairless head and flabby face of Mr. Hillbury peering out

'Good evening, Mr. Hillbury,' he said pleasantly. 'I'm afraid rather an unfortunate thing has happened. One of your servants has been murdered.'

'Murdered!' The high voice was a shrill squeak, and the big face twitched in terror.

'How did it happen? Who did it?'

Jim told him as briefly as possible.

'My God, how dreadful,' whispered Mr. Hillbury. 'Go up to the house, Cusher, and telephone. At once do you hear?

The man with the automatic hesitated, and then, shrugging his shoulders, he shoved the weapon into his pocket and moved towards the wicket. The stout man insinuated his huge body with difficulty through the gate and came to Jim's side.

'Must have been a burglar,' he said shakily. 'Some man got into the grounds — '

'Your servant was killed by somebody called Queer Face,' interrupted Jim, and the stout man reeled.

'Queer Face!' he exclaimed shrilly, his face the colour of putty.

'How do you know that? How do you

know anything about Queer Face?' He was shaking as though he had ague and his flaccid cheeks were wet and shiny.

'Your man spoke before he died,' answered Jim. 'He said he did it. 'Queer Face'. Do you know whom he meant?'

By a desperate effort Mr. Hillbury regained something of composure.

'No, no,' he replied quickly. 'I can only suggest the poor fellow was delirious. I don't know anything, how should I?' His voice trailed away incoherently and he glanced uneasily towards the patch of thickly-grown trees at the side of the road.

The man was in the last stages of terror; it was visible in his eyes and in the nervous twitching of his small mouth and in the tremulous, almost hysterical voice. 'I thought the name seemed rather to upset you,' said Jim, quietly.

'Upset me?' quavered Mr. Hillbury. 'Isn't this enough to upset anybody? It's dreadful . . . terrible . . . ' He took a handkerchief from a pocket of his dressing gown — Jim saw that beneath the garment he was clad in his pyjamas

— and wiped his face. 'The shock has unnerved me,' he said with a ghastly attempt at a smile. 'I'm afraid my heart is a little weak and any excitement is bad for it.'

A silence fell between them that was broken by the return of the servant.

'I got through to the police station,' he said a little breathlessly, as though he had been running, 'B-b-but Superintendent Laker wasn't there. I told 'em what had happened though, and they're gettin' 'old of 'im and sending up right away.'

'Good,' said Jim.

'I think, if you don't mind, I'll go back to the house,' said Mr. Hillbury, nervously. 'If you require any — any assistance at all — ' He hesitated, at a loss to complete the sentence.

'I've no doubt that Superintendent Laker will want to see you later,' said Jim. 'And you too,' he added looking at the man Cusher. That individual growled something under his breath and turned away to accompany his master. When he was alone Jim strolled over to the fringe of the patch of trees and stared at the gloomy depths of the little copse. It was useless examining it for any traces of the murderer, for he had no torch with him and the darkness was intense. It was one of the things he had not brought with him on his holiday, never thinking that he would be in need of it.

He wondered what was the real cause of Mr. Hillbury's fear and why the stout man had taken such elaborate precautions guard his house against the possible visit of a night marauder. That he had done so was obvious from the trip wire Jim had stumbled over and the floodlight that had been fixed to the side of the house to illumine the grounds. It was also pretty evident that the two men he had selected for his servants had been chosen more for their qualifications as a body-guard than anything else. There was a touch of the ex-pugilist about both of them. That the fat man was in deadly fear of someone, Jim was certain, and that that someone was the man with the peculiar face seemed equally obvious.

But how did the girl come into it, the girl who had screamed? Was it because of her presence in the house that Hillbury was scared? Was the unknown man who had been lurking in the woods and who had killed Dan, in some way connected with the girl who called herself Lesley Allerton?

Jim stared up at the star-sprinkled sky; it looked as though his holiday had come to an abrupt end, for he had no intention of leaving Siltley until he had discovered exactly what was happening at Dead Trees.

The hum of a car in the distance attracted his attention as presently he saw the lights coming along the road. It slowed, and came to a halt a few yards away and as Jim walked towards them. Superintendent Laker, a uniformed police-man, and a round-faced little man got out. Laker had evidently dressed hurriedly for the collar of a pyjama jacket showed above his big coat. He listened without comment while Jim briefly told his story, and then going over stared down at the huddled figure of the dead man.

'H'm,' he muttered. 'Queer Face, eh? Sounds like something out of a sensa-tional story. I suppose we can't put too much reliance on this fellow's words though, he may have been a bit delirious.'

Jim said nothing. Privately he thought that the man had been very sane, but he did not stress the point. He had said nothing of his vision of the man in the wood, nor of his adventures in the grounds of Dead Trees. That, from an official standpoint, would require a great deal of explaining away, and he had let the Superintendent think that he had merely been out for a walk and was passing the gate when the crime had been committed.

'You carry on, Doctor, will you,' said Laker turning to the round-faced little man. 'Fetch me the inspection lamp from the car, Miller.'

The constable went over to the car and presently came back with an electric lamp attached to a long length of flex, and by its light the police doctor made a careful examination of the man on the ground.

'Stabbed in the throat,' he muttered. 'A pretty bad wound too, must have severed the jugular.' He looked up. 'I'd like the knife removed.'

Laker bent down, and taking a handkerchief from his pocket wrapped it round the hilt of the weapon. He had some difficulty in pulling it out, but he succeeded and looked at the razor-sharp discoloured blade in the light of the lamp held by the constable.

'Nothing very special about it,' he grunted disappointedly. 'You can buy them by the hundred in any shop that sells this sort of thing. Perhaps the hilt will tell us something when we dust it for prints.'

He wrapped the knife carefully in his handkerchief and stowed it away in his breast pocket. There was a silence while they watched the little doctor finish his examination.

'I can't tell you very much,' he announced presently, rising to his feet and brushing the knees of his trousers. 'At least, nothing to prove helpful. The man was stabbed in the throat and the knife severed the big arteries. He couldn't have lived more than a few minutes after receiving the blow.'

'As you say, that doesn't help us much,'

remarked Laker. 'We'll go up to the house now and have a word with Mr. Hillbury. If you like to wait in the car, Doctor, you can come back with us, I don't suppose we shall be very long.'

He went over to the drive gates, accompanied by Jim, and rang the bell. Cusher had evidently taken up his stand just inside, for the wicket gate opened almost immediately and his unprepossessing face peered out. Recognising Jim he stepped aside to let them enter, closing and rebolting the wicket immediately they had passed through.

Mr. Hillbury was pacing up and down the big hall but there was no sign of his wife. She had either slept throughout the events of the night or he had taken the precaution of keeping her out of the way. His perturbation had abated somewhat and he was almost calm as he ushered them into a small room leading off the hall that was furnished in the semblance of an office.

'The man's name was Killick,' he said in answer to Laker's question. 'Daniel Killick. I know very little about him except that he was an ex-prize fighter and an excellent servant. But that he should have met his death in my employ is tragic — tragic.'

'It would have been equally tragic for him whoever he'd been employed by,' said Jim shortly, and Mr. Hillbury agreed with a sickly smile.

'I should like you to tell me, sir, exactly what happened here tonight,' said the Superintendent.

It was an unsatisfactory interview, and after questioning Cusher, who bore out his master's statement almost word for word, Laker and Jim took their departure, no wiser than when they had come.

They found that the ambulance had been during their absence and taken away the body of the dead servant, and with it the police doctor.

Leaving the constable on duty, they drove back to the station house at Little Siltley, and in the privacy of his small office Laker took out the knife, and unwrapping it laid it on his blotting pad.

'Perhaps this will tell us something,' he said. 'I'm going to bring out the fingerprints if there are any.'

He went over to his cupboard and returned with a small bottle half filled with a fine white powder. Shaking a little of this on to the black hilt of the knife he agitated it gently until the wooden handle was covered with a white film of dust. When he blew the residue away several prints were visible.

'That's something, anyway,' he said with satisfaction. 'The murderer didn't wear gloves.'

But Jim did not hear him. He was staring fascinated at the knife-handle, his heart pumping wildly, for the white powder had brought out with startling distinctness, a thumbprint, and it was the thumbprint of his father's murderer.

7

A Shot From a Car

Jim looked at the thumbprint, hardly believing the evidence of his senses, and yet he was so familiar with every loop, and whorl that he knew that he could not be mistaken. This was a replica of the print that had been found on the polished handle of the motor launch. He had examined the photograph during the last three years so often that he could almost have drawn it from memory.

Laker looked at the white, strained face of the man before him anxiously. 'What's the matter, Mr. Brent?' he asked. 'Do you recognise that print?'

Jim nodded. For the moment he found it impossible to speak, his throat was dry with the shock of the discovery. For three years he had hoped vainly to match the thumbprint that had been found on the gear lever, and now his hope had been realised.

'Yes,' he said huskily at length, and even to himself his voice sounded unlike his own. 'I recognise it.'

The Superintendent looked interested.

'If they've got a record of that print at the Yard,' he said, 'it should be easy — '

'They haven't,' broke in Jim, shaking his head. 'At least they've got a record of it but they don't know to whom it belongs.' He passed his tongue over his dry lips. 'Do you remember a series of jewel robberies three years ago!'

Laker nodded.

'I read about them,' he replied.

'The perpetrator was never caught,' continued Jim looking at him steadily. 'My father was in charge of the case and he laid a trap for him. The man walked into it, but succeeded in getting away after killing my father. He shot him at point blank range, and the only clue he left behind him was a thumbprint on the gear lever of the launch he used.' He pointed with a hand that was not quite steady at the knife on Laker's desk.

'That's it,' he ended shortly.

The Superintendent looked at him incredulously. 'Are you sure you haven't made a mistake,' he began, but Jim cut him short.

'No I've made no mistake,' he answered grimly. I know that print as well as I know the back of my own hand. The man who killed Daniel Killick and the man who killed my father are one and the same.'

'Well, it's amazing,' said Laker. 'But I don't see that it helps us very much.'

'It doesn't,' replied Jim, 'but it makes me all the keener to get him. I swore three years ago, Laker, that one day I'd get him, and I've always known that I should. It gives me a special interest in this business to know that the man who shot my father is somewhere in the neighbourhood.'

'I suppose you're absolutely sure, Mr. Brent?' he said, 'It's very easy to make a mistake over a thumbprint.'

'Not over this one,' retorted Jim, and thrusting his hand into his breast pocket he withdrew a wallet.

Searching among its contents he took out an envelope. Opening the flap and putting in his thumb and finger he brought to light a square, glossy print. He laid it down on the blotting pad in front of Laker and the Superintendent bent forward.

'If you have any doubts,' said Jim, 'compare the two.' The Superintendent did so, carefully.

'No, there's no doubt,' he remarked presently. 'You were right, they're one and the same.'

Jim picked up the photograph and replaced it carefully in his pocketbook.

'You know Laker,' he said suddenly, 'the Yard will have to come into this now. This print will bring them into it because it belongs to a man they've been looking for, for years.'

'Yes, I suppose so,' said Laker a little dubiously.

Jim guessed from the expression on the Superintendent's face, what was passing in his mind and to a certain extent sympathised with him. This was one of the few chances that had ever come the man's way and it was more than hard to see it snatched from under his nose.

'I tell you what,' he said. 'I'll get on to the Yard first thing in the morning, tell them what has happened and explain that I'm already on the spot. In the circumstances they're pretty sure to let me carry on, and, apart altogether from personal considerations, I must say I'm interested in the business. You'd rather work with me than a stranger, wouldn't you?'

'I would, Mr. Brent,' declared Laker, and his lugubrious expression visibly brightened.

'Well, that's that then,' said Jim. 'I'll get on to Chief Inspector Mason first thing in the morning. In the meanwhile we'd better lock that knife up somewhere. Tomorrow I'll pack it up and send it to London with the photograph.'

'I'll put it in here,' said the Superintendent, and rising to his feet, he took a key from his pocket, crossed over to a safe in one corner of his office and unlocked it.

Coming back to his desk he picked up the knife gingerly by the discoloured blade, carried it over to the safe, and laying it on an empty space on one of the shelves, shut and relocked the door.

'I think that's all we can do for tonight,' said Jim, suppressing a yawn. 'I'll get back to the inn and come round and see you immediately after breakfast.'

He was feeling suddenly dog tired, and apart from this, longed for the seclusion of his bedroom, where he could sort out the jumble of thoughts that were running chaotically through his brain. Laker, who was not averse to getting back to his own bed, agreed with the suggestion, and wishing him good night Jim left the station house and turned in the direction of the Load of Hay.

The inn lay on the outskirts of the village and to reach it he had to walk the whole length of the deserted High Street.

The night was very still, and although from the lightening of the sky in the east the dawn could not be far off, it still retained something of its earlier sultriness.

The little shops and cottages on either side of the narrow street were dark and lifeless, and Jim's lips curled in a slight smile as he thought of the inhabitants sleeping peacefully, unaware of the tragedy that had occurred almost in their midst.

Murder had stalked abroad that night amidst those tranquil, scented lawns. Murder in the guise of a man with a white and shapeless face, whose hands were previously stained with the blood of an old man who had been butchered in the execution of his duty.

'Queer Face,' muttered Jim softly as he strode along and wondered what was the secret of that peculiar puffy whiteness that he had glimpsed for a moment in the cigarette glow in the heart of the little wood. Was it a disguise — something the man had applied to his face in order to conceal his identity — or was it some form of physical disease, a dreadful ailment that had ravaged that face and turned it into a loathsome, inhuman mask.

He was so immersed in his thoughts that he failed to hear the smooth running car that came speeding along the road behind him until it was almost on him, and then the headlights reflected on the side of a cottage in front warned him of its nearness and he stepped out of the roadway on to the narrow pavement to let it pass. It swept by him, a long low saloon. He looked at it disinterestedly, and then, from the interior leaped a red pencil of flame and without a sound, Jim Brent crumpled in a heap on the sidewalk.

8

Two Visitors from Fleet Street

Jim recovered his senses and staggered unsteadily to his feet; his head was aching furiously and something warm was running down his face into his collar. He was feeling rather sick and dizzy and leaned against the fence of one of the little cottage gardens to recover. Putting up his hand, he felt the side of his head gingerly, and discovered a long, narrow wound that ran from his right temple to just behind his ear. It was bleeding freely, but luckily did not seem to be serious. The bullet had apparently just grazed the side of his head, the shock being sufficient to stun him momentarily.

With a rather shaky hand he felt for his cigarette case and lighted a cigarette. He had seen that spear of flame leap out from the interior of the car, but he had heard no sound. The shooter, whoever it was, had been using a pistol fitted with a silencer. He propped himself up against the little fence and puffed at his cigarette. Gradually the nausea and faintness began to wear off. Somebody evidently disliked his presence in Little Siltley. The question was, who? Was it Queer Face who had shot at him from the interior of that car, or one of the mysterious inhabitants of Dead Trees.

He dabbed at his wound with his handkerchief, and presently found that the bleeding had ceased.

The sky was lightening rapidly, and glancing at his watch Jim saw that it was a quarter to four. Most of the night was gone, and if he wanted to get any sleep at all before starting on the busy day that lay ahead of him he concluded that he had better be making a move.

Except for an unpleasant headache, he was feeling almost his normal self as he continued on his way to the inn. He succeeded in reaching his bedroom by way of the window and the lean-to shed without attracting attention, and after bathing and dressing the wound in his temple he slipped off his clothes and crawled into bed with a sigh of relief.

He fell asleep almost at once, and did not wake until the buxom maid knocked at his door with his morning tea. He felt no ill effects from his wound beyond a slight soreness of the head, and dressing, he went down to the coffee-room.

He had finished his breakfast and was lingering over a final cup of coffee when he heard the squeak of brakes as a car drew up outside the inn, followed presently by a cheery voice demanding breakfast. Jim started, for the voice was familiar, and a little later, when its owner appeared at the door of the coffee-room, he saw that he had not been mistaken.

'Good morning, Kemp,' he said, with a grin. 'What are you doing in this neighbourhood?'

The newcomer stared and then his large, red face broke into a grin of recognition.

'Jimmy Brent, by the toenail of Methuselah's pet monkey!' he exclaimed, and twisting his head he called over his shoulder: 'Phil. I say, Phil, come here.'

He advanced to where Jim was sitting, held out a huge hand and crushed the other's fingers in a grip that made him wince.

'What is it, Freddy?' asked a clear voice, and a girl came into the room.

'It's me, Miss Orde,' said Jim, rising to his feet.

The girl's eyes widened in surprise.

'Why, Mr. Brent,' she said. 'What are you doing here?'

Jim laughed.

'I might ask you the same thing,' he answered. 'What has brought the cream of Fleet Street journalism to this small and uninteresting village so early in the morning?'

'Business,' said Freddy Kemp, with a wave of his massive hand. 'Business, old boy. We're on the job, aren't we, Phil?'

The girl nodded, and Jim looked from one to the other, his face puckered in a puzzled expression.

'Well, that's pretty quick work,' he remarked. 'How in the world did you come to hear of the murder so soon?'

'Murder?' repeated Kemp, 'What murder?'

The puzzled expression on Jim's face deepened.

'Do you mean it wasn't the murder that brought you here?' he demanded, and it was Phyllis Orde who answered him.

'We know nothing about a murder, Mr. Brent,' she said seriously. 'We're here on quite a different matter.'

'We have, in fact,' put in Freddy Kemp, 'come down at the behest of an imaginative editor, to secure an interview with Dr. Patterson-Willis.'

Jim thought the name sounded vaguely familiar, but for the moment he was unable to remember in what connection.

'Who the deuce is Dr. Patterson-Willis?' he asked.

'Dr. Patterson-Willis,' explained Kemp, oratorically, 'is the famous authority on skin diseases. His long suit is leprosy. He has just come back from abroad, to be exact from the leper colony at — Why, what's the matter, man?'

He broke off at the sight of the sudden change that had come over Jim's face.

'Nothing,' muttered Jim. 'Go on.'

But although Kemp complied, he only

heard a word here and there of what he said. Once more, he was looking into the darkness of the little wood by the high wall surrounding Dead Trees, once more he saw the red glow of the cigarette, and the white puffiness of that dreadful face which had been momentarily revealed to him. Leprosy! That would account for it — for that inhuman mask that had stared at him out of the darkness of the wood.

Queer Face was a leper!

The deep droning of Freddy Kemp's voice ceased abruptly, and Jim roused himself from his reverie.

'Where does this Dr. Patterson-Willis live?' he asked.

The big journalist looked at him curiously and slowly shook his head.

'I've just been telling you,' he answered pityingly, 'but I suppose you weren't listening. What's the matter with you, old man? Have you fallen for some buxom country wench? Or is it indigestion?'

'It's neither,' said Jim. 'It's merely that I'm occupied with rather a knotty little problem at the moment, and what you've told me about Patterson-Willis seems to fit in remarkably well.'

'With the murder, do you mean?' asked the girl quickly, and Jim nodded.

'We seem,' said Freddy Kemp, delightedly, 'to have struck something. I scent a story. Tell us all about it, old boy.'

Jim hesitated.

'I will if you'll promise me,' he said after a moment's pause, 'that you won't use it.'

Kemp looked at him reproachfully.

'How long have you known me?' he said. 'Getting on for six years, isn't it? And you say a thing like that. I'm surprised at you, Inspector Brent. Have I ever printed anything that was told me in confidence?'

'Yes,' said Jim truthfully, and his friend laughed.

'Candid but unkind,' he said. 'However, in this case you need have no fear. I promise you I'll publish nothing without your permission.'

At that moment the rosy-faced waitress entered with a tray containing the breakfast that Kemp had ordered, and they waited until she had set it on the table and taken her departure. When they were once more alone, and had gathered round the table Jim began an account of all that had happened since his arrival at Little Siltley on the previous day. Both Kemp and the girl listened interestedly, making no comment until he had finished.

'Phil,' said Freddy Kemp, when Jim concluded, 'we're in luck. We came down here on a rather prosaic interview, and we've fallen into the middle of a real, bang, slap-up, front-page story, the answer to a reporter's prayer. It's great stuff.'

'Only we can't use it,' murmured his pretty companion.

'We can use some of it,' declared Kemp. 'You've no objection to that, have you, Jim? I mean the murder is bound to become public property, and the *Clarion* may as well be the first to come with it.'

'As long as you don't mention anything about the thumbprint, the dead man's last words, and the fellow I saw in the woods,' answered Jim, 'you can do what you like.'

'Fine,' said Freddy. 'I'll get on to old Pops at once — as soon as we've finished breakfast and I can find the telephone.'

'There's a telephone in the Post Office, in the High Street,' said Jim. 'About five minutes away from here.'

'Good,' said Freddy. 'I've no doubt Pops will want me to stop and cover the affair. If he does, what about working together?'

'That suits me,' said Jim, and in fact he would rather have had the assistance of Freddy Kemp than any experienced man from Scotland Yard, for in spite of his somewhat bovine exterior the journalist possessed a keen brain and, moreover, would be a useful ally in a tight corner, for he had a punch like an ox and knew as much about the finer arts of boxing as a professional pugilist.

The *Clarion* possessed a special 'crime man' of its own, but more often than not it was Kemp who got the story, and with the supreme good nature that was part of his character, turned it over to his confrère to appear under that gentleman's name.

He knew nearly everybody who was anybody. Was a welcome visitor at Scotland Yard; attended all the first-nights, where on occasions he would deputise for the dramatic critic; was seen at most of the big race meetings, and spent a thoroughly enjoyable life, having the knack of making his amusements pay for themselves over and over again.

It was generally supposed that he and Phyllis Orde were engaged, though neither of them had confirmed the rumour. At the same time they had not denied it, and this was accepted as a tacit admission amongst their friends and acquaintances.

He had met the girl when she had been struggling to earn a precarious living as a free lance, having given up a job on an obscure provincial newspaper in order to come up and seek her fortune in London. He had succeeded in getting her a job on the *Clarion*, and when she was not engaged on other work she acted as a sort of unofficial secretary and assistant to him.

She possessed an amazing memory,

could repeat almost word for word a long conversation or any special bit of information that was told her, and he found her amazingly helpful. She was a small girl, with a neat, trim figure and a face that if it could not be called exactly pretty was so animated and held such a sweet expression that it was infinitely more satisfying to look upon than mere physical beauty. Her eyes were really lovely, big and brown and capable of expressing an amazing variety of emotions. By the side of her enormous companion she looked tiny and fragile, but in reality was of normal height and far stronger than the average girl of her age and build.

When they had finished breakfast they went out to Kemp's disreputable looking car, and all three drove down to the Post Office in the High Street.

The journalist had some difficulty in getting through to the *Clarion*, but he succeeded eventually, and when he rejoined Jim and the girl his face was wreathed in smiles.

'Everything's O.K.,' he announced.

'I'm staying down here to cover this murder business, and I've got permission for you to help me.' He grinned at the girl and looked at Jim. 'What's the next move?' he demanded.

'I'm going to get on to Scotland Yard,' said Jim. 'After that, if you'll run me down to the police station I'll introduce you both to Superintendent Laker, and then, if you're calling on Dr. Patterson-Willis, I'd like to come with you.'

Kemp shot him a shrewd glance.

'What's your interest in Patterson-Willis?' he asked.

'Leprosy,' answered Jim shortly, and went over to the telephone to put his call through.

Chief-Inspector Mason had just arrived, and he listened with interest to Jim's account of the murder and the mystery he had stumbled upon.

'If that thumbprint is the same,' was his comment, 'you're on to something big. Carry on, and if you want any help let me know.'

They met Laker just ascending the steps of the station house, and Jim introduced Kemp and the girl.

The Superintendent appeared a little displeased at the intrusion of a newspaper reporter into the affair, but his displeasure was quickly dispelled by his astonishment, when Jim questioned him concerning Patterson-Willis.

'I know him by sight,' he said, 'but not to speak to. He lives at Lady's Manor, about two hundred yards from Dead Trees, on the other side of the little wood. At one time it was all one property. Before Dead Trees was converted into an asylum it used to be the big house in these parts. I didn't know the doctor was back, he can't have been very long.'

'He hasn't,' put in Kemp. 'He only came back from abroad last week.'

'I suppose he spends most of his time away,' said Jim, and Laker nodded.

'Yes,' he answered. 'If he's back now, it's the first time for two years.' He looked at Jim curiously and wrinkled his forehead. 'Why are you so interested in him, Mr. Brent?'

'He sounds rather an abnormal person,' answered Jim evasively, 'and I'm always interested in abnormal people.'

'I see,' said Laker, but the tone of his voice was unconvinced and he eyed Jim rather sharply, as though at the back of his mind he had an idea that the young Inspector was keeping something from him.

'How did you manage to hurt yourself, Mr. Brent?' he said suddenly, as he caught sight of the strip of plaster on Jim's temple.

'I didn't; it was done for me,' answered Jim grimly. 'It's only a scratch, but it might easily have proved fatal.'

He told the Superintendent about the shots from the car, and Laker's eyes widened.

'By Jove!' he exclaimed. 'Somebody didn't lose much time in trying to put you out of the running! I suppose you can't give anything in the nature of a description of the car?'

Jim shook his head.

'I'm afraid I can't,' he replied, 'except that it was a big saloon and was painted either black or dark blue, which isn't likely to help much.'

84

'No, but I'll make inquiries all the same,' said the Superintendent. 'Are you going up to Lady's Manor now?'

'That was the intention,' said Jim. 'By the way, I've been on to the Yard and fixed things up. They told me to carry on, and I said we were sending the knife up to be photographed. Will you do that?'

Laker nodded and looked at his watch.

'There's just time to pack up before I go to see the Chief Constable,' he said. 'I'll post it on my way.'

He stood watching them as they drove off, and then, pursing his lips dubiously, disappeared inside the police station.

What was the meaning behind this sudden interest in Dr. Patterson-Willis? If this fellow Brent thought Willis had anything to do with the affair at Dead Trees he was wasting his time. Patterson-Willis had lived in Little Siltley, on and off, for years, and couldn't have any connection with Hillbury or the man who had been killed, or for that matter with the jewel robber whose thumbprint had been found on the hilt of the knife. And yet there was something at the back of

Brent's mind; that explanation about being interested in abnormal people was all my eye and Betty Martin.

Laker's expression was very thoughtful as he took the knife from the safe and carefully packed it up. He didn't know it then, but Dr. Willis was to take a leading part in the events that were to come, and by his own unaided efforts clear up the mystery surrounding Dead Trees and the identity of the killer of Mr. Hillsbury's servant.

9

At Lady's Manor

'I don't want this fellow, Patterson-Willis, to know who I am,' said Jim as they drove along. 'Just let him think I'm a friend of yours.'

Without taking his eyes off the road ahead Freddy Kemp nodded.

'All right,' he said. 'I'll let him think you're a member of the great ink-fingered brigade. I gathered from your reticence with the Superintendent that you haven't told him anything about the queer-faced gentleman.'

'You gathered rightly,' said Jim. 'I haven't mentioned him yet. I want to know a little more about him before I do.'

'Don't you think your idea is a little far-fetched?' said Phyllis Orde, and Jim twisted round in his seat to face her. 'I mean that this man is a leper. Even if Dr. Willis had brought anyone suffering from such a horrible disease back with him, he would scarcely allow him to wander loose about the countryside.'

'No,' said Jim. 'But all the same, you must admit it's an extraordinary coincidence. There undoubtedly is something wrong with this fellow I saw, and leprosy, from what I've heard of it, would fit his appearance exactly.'

'It's certainly queer,' said the girl. 'But I don't see how it can be anything more than a coincidence — that Patterson-Willis is an authority on leprosy. This man whom you saw lurking about in the wood and who killed Daniel Killick is the same man, according to your idea, who was responsible for the series of jewel robberies three years ago!'

'That's right,' said Jim nodding. 'I don't think there's any doubt of it.'

'Well, then, how could Dr. Patterson have brought him back from abroad,' argued the girl.

'I don't think that's an objection,' said Jim. 'After he escaped that night at Bourne End he completely vanished. Nobody knows where he went to. He could quite easily have gone abroad and contracted leprosy.'

'I'm not an authority on the subject,' she answered, 'but I doubt if it could have reached such a serious stage as you describe in the time.'

'Another thing,' broke in Freddy Kemp. 'Why should he want to get into the grounds of this fellow Hillbury's home, and what motive could he have for murdering the servant?'

'If I could tell you that,' said Jim, 'the business would be practically over. I'm willing to admit that I don't know — any more than I know who Lesley Allerton is and why the Hillburys are holding her a prisoner.'

'If they are,' grunted the journalist. 'Hillbury may have been speaking the truth. Perhaps his wife does have attacks of lunacy.'

Jim shook his head.

'No,' he declared. 'I'm convinced that there's another woman somewhere in the house; that's the only explanation for the perfume I smelt in the hall.'

'Well, it's a real nice, juicy problem,'

chuckled Freddy Kemp. 'I haven't struck anything so interesting for months, and I'm jolly glad we came down.'

He gave a twist to the wheel, and turned the car sharply into a narrow lane. It bumped and rattled over the uneven surface, and it was with a sigh of relief that he brought it to a halt in front of two crumbling stone pillars that supported a rusty iron gate.

'I'm glad we haven't far to go along this way,' he grunted as he slid from the driving seat to the roadway. 'A few more yards of this and the old bus would have shaken to pieces.'

'About the best thing that could happen to it,' said Jim unkindly. 'Why don't you get a respectable car?'

'This car's deceiving,' said Freddy Kemp. 'It doesn't look much, I admit, but it can do seventy at a pinch, and I haven't had to pay a repair bill for eighteen months.'

He looked at the entrance to Lady's Manor and scratched his chin.

'Doesn't look much of a place, does it?' he remarked, eyeing the gloomy tunnel of the drive which could be seen through the iron gates.

Jim agreed with him.

The house could not be seen at all from the gate. It was completely hidden by the screen of trees into which the drive twisted and was lost. Jim went over, and grasping the latch of the iron gate attempted to push it open. He had to apply nearly all his strength before it moved, and when it did it swung grudgingly and to the accompaniment of a protesting squeal from the rusty hinges.

'We'd better leave the car here, hadn't we,' said Freddy Kemp, and such was the atmosphere of the place that he involuntarily spoke in a whisper as though afraid to raise his voice.

Jim nodded.

'Yes, we can walk up to the house,' he replied.

They set off with the girl between them, their feet swishing through the riotous weeds that covered the driveway. Here in the tunnel of the elms it was like twilight. No ray from the sun above penetrated the thick canopy of leaves, and a humid chill seemed to arise from the ground as they proceeded. Presently, as they came round the bend, they got their first glimpse of the house.

It was a low, rambling building, built of the same grey stone as the wall. A circle of neglected lawn, from the centre of which rose an enormous cypress tree, stretched in front of the pillared portico. Behind and on either side of this desolate abode were more trees, forming a roughly shaped horseshoe. The stillness here was still profound; there was no movement or sign to show that the house was occupied.

No wonder, thought Jim, as he looked at it, that Dr Patterson-Willis spent most of his time abroad. To live long in this gloomy residence would be sufficient to give anyone suicidal mania.

'Shall I knock or ring, or whatever one does?' asked Freddy.

'Yes, I think you'd better,' replied Jim. 'You're the fellow that's got the appointment with the owner. If there is an owner,' he added doubtfully, looking at the apparently deserted mansion before him.

The journalist made no answer, but ascending the steps he searched round for some means of warning the inhabitants of their presence. There was no knocker, but at the side of the heavy oak door he found an old-fashioned iron bell-pull. Raising his hand he gave it a tug, and from somewhere inside the house came a discordant clamour. It died away to silence, and then without warning the door was suddenly jerked open and a huge black man stood on the threshold staring at them.

'What d'you want?' he demanded ungraciously.

Freddy Kemp produced a card.

'I wish to see Dr. Patterson-Willis,' he said. 'I'm from the *Clarion*, and I have an appointment with him.'

The man took the card, looked at it, shot a quick glance at each one of them in turn, and then with a muttered 'Wait,' vanished into the shadow of the hall.

Kemp turned to Jim with a grimace.

'Nice cheery reception,' he muttered. 'Pleasant sort of fellow.'

Jim said nothing, but all his senses were

93

alert and watchful. He felt there was something wrong with this house. That behind the silence and the gloom and the neglect was something sinister. The same sensation had attacked him once before when he had gone into an apparently respectable club in Tottenham Court Road and later discovered that it served as a mask for the activities of a gang of dope peddlers.

The black man came back, no longer holding the card, and held the door open wider.

'You come this way,' he said, and Freddy Kemp stepped across the threshold into the hall.

Jim and Phyllis Orde followed him, and the big man closed the door behind them with a bang.

When it was shut the hall was almost in complete darkness. Two narrow, slit-like windows on either side of the entrance provided the only light, and the glass of these was so grimy that the feeble glimmer that came through only served to accentuate the gloom. They could just make out the huge figure of their guide as he crossed to a door on the left and knocked. A shaft of light streamed out as he turned the handle and opened it, silhouetting his figure and throwing a long shadow across the carpeted floor. He beckoned and stood aside for them to enter.

The room into which they were ushered was large and furnished as a library. Every available foot of wall space was occupied by laden bookcases. The volumes were nearly all old, some of them almost falling to pieces, and from them came a strange musty odour, a mingling of old leather and paper. A thick carpet covered the floor, and in the centre of the room was an enormous black-topped table littered with books and papers. Except for this there was very little furniture. A couple of ancient leather armchairs drawn up to the fireless grate, and a small table on which stood a tray containing a coffee pot and a cup and saucer.

At the writing table a man was seated reading a newspaper. He looked up as they entered, and Jim thought he had seldom come in contact with such an unusual personality. He was clean-shaven, and rather on the thin side. His hair, brushed back from his forehead, was grey, with strands of white that gave it a peculiar striped appearance. His complexion was very dark, the complexion of a man who has spent much of his life under tropical suns, and his eyes, deep set beneath overhanging brows, were of an uncommon shade of grey that was almost the colour of smoke. He looked at them steadily, but said nothing, and it was Freddy Kemp who was the first to speak.

'Dr. Patterson-Willis?' he asked politely.

'Yes,' he answered. 'You're the man from the *Clarion*, aren't you? Sit down,' he went on, 'and tell me as quickly as you can what I can do for you.'

Freddy Kemp crossed over and took up his position in front of the grate.

'My paper is rather keen on printing an interview with you,' he said presently. 'I daresay they told you that when the appointment was made.'

Dr. Willis nodded without looking at him; his gaze was fixed on Jim and the girl, who had remained standing by the door.

Seeing his interest the journalist hastened to introduce them.

'This is Mr. Pillbottle,' he said, jerking his head at Jim. 'One of the most brilliant men on our staff; and my secretary, Miss Orde.'

'Does it usually take three of you to secure an interview?' he asked sharply, and it seemed to Jim a trifle suspiciously.

Freddy Kemp was equal to the occasion.

'Not as a rule,' he said easily, 'but in this case, where there is likely to be quite a lot of technical matter, the editor thought it best.'

'H'm!' said the man at the table. 'Well, I'm sorry you should have all your trouble for nothing. I've changed my mind, Mr. — er' — he dropped his eyes to the card in front of him — 'Mr. Kemp. I'm afraid I cannot give you the interview you require.'

Freddy Kemp looked a little taken aback.

'But I thought it was all arranged,' he said. 'I was told — '

'I believe I did agree to something of

the sort,' agreed Dr. Patterson-Willis. 'But as I said, I've changed my mind. I don't require anything in the nature of publicity at the moment.'

'Oh, come, Doctor,' said Kemp persuasively. 'Now that we're here — '

'Now that you're here,' broke in the other again, rising to his feet, 'I must, at the risk of appearing rude, ask you to go. I am extremely busy at the moment and my time is very valuable. Good morning.'

He walked across to the door and held it open. They could do nothing but leave with as good a grace as possible. The black man met them in the hall and escorted them to the front door, barely waiting for them to pass through before he closed it behind them.

'Well that's that,' said Freddy Kemp when they stood once more at the foot of the steps. 'What you might call the polite chuck out. That fellow is certainly pretty quick at changing his mind.'

'Did he promise to give you an interview?' asked Jim.

'So I understood from Pops,' answered the journalist. 'He told me that it was all arranged and that all I'd got to do was to come down and get the copy. I must get on the phone when we get back and tell them at the office.'

'I wonder why he changed his mind,' said Phyllis Orde thoughtfully.

'Oh, these scientific fellows are all alike,' grunted Freddy. 'I suppose he's just feeling liverish or something. Whatever it was, we appear to have wasted our time, unless you saw anything helpful.' he added, turning to Jim.

'I didn't,' answered Jim shaking his head. 'Still I'm glad to have met the man though I don't think — ' he stopped abruptly, expelling his breath with a little hissing gasp.

'What's up?' asked Kemp.

They had reached the beginning of the drive and while they had been speaking Jim had turned to take a last look at the gloomy house they had just left.

'Look there,' he said quickly. 'At the window above the porch.'

Freddy Kemp looked.

'I can't see anything,' he grunted. 'What's all the excitement about?'

'There isn't anything — now,' retorted Jim, 'But there was.'

For an instant, peering at them through the grimy glass, he had glimpsed a face, white, shapeless, puffy, the face of the man he had seen in the cigarette glow lurking in the wood on the night of Dan Killick's murder.

10

The Voice on the Telephone

Mr. Hillbury carefully cracked an egg, removed a small portion of the shell, and stared gloomily at his handiwork. It was not that there was anything wrong with the egg, it was in excellent condition; the trouble lay in Mr. Hillbury's mind. He was a man greatly worried, and if the truth must be told, badly frightened. The murder of his servant on the previous night had been a shock from which he had not yet recovered. A still greater shock lay in Dan's last words to Jim Brent.

Although not unexpected, the confirmation of his worst fears had come as a staggering blow. His enemy was at hand; at any moment might strike at him as he had struck at the little prizefighter. In spite of all Mr. Hillbury's precautions he had, in some inexplicable manner succeeded in getting into the grounds of

Dead Trees. But for the alarm bell having rung and warned them of his presence anything might have happened. The fat man shivered.

He had no idea that the alarm bell had been set ringing by Jim Brent for he was unaware of the young Inspector's presence as an unauthorised intruder in his grounds. Had he known that, his fears would have been increased.

He presented an unpleasant picture as he slowly ate his breakfast. A faded silk dressing gown enveloped his ample form and he had neither washed nor shaved. A reddish stubble covered his many chins and threw into relief the pasty sallowness of his face. Pouches of skin hung beneath his tired eyes and the corners of his loose mouth drooped pathetically.

He looked up as Cusher came into the room.

'I've found out how that fellow got in,' grunted the man. 'He climbed the wall from the lane and used an old arch as a ladder.'

Knowing nothing of Jim Brent's excursion, he had, like Mr. Hillbury, fallen into the error that the arch had been placed there by the other unknown intruder.

Mr. Hillbury frowned.

'We must take extra precautions, George,' he said. 'The grounds must be patrolled at night from now on. You'd better arrange it with Sam.'

Cusher looked at him curiously.

'Who is this fellow you're afraid of?' he asked.

'I've told you,' said Mr. Hillbury. 'He's an old business associate of mine who fancies he has a grievance against me and being a little mad he's dangerous.'

'I can't see why you don't let him get in,' said Cusher. 'You and me and Sam can tackle 'im and put 'im where 'e couldn't do no further 'arm.'

The spoon, which had been conveying a portion of egg to Mr. Hillbury's capacious mouth dropped, and he started.

'That is a suggestion, George,' he said thoughtfully. 'Yes, that is certainly a suggestion, I will turn it over in my mind. How's the girl this morning?'

'She's all right,' grunted George. 'I've just taken her breakfast. Sam's looking after her.'

'She must be carefully guarded,'

warned his master. 'On no account must she be allowed outside the house.'

'It would be a bloomin' miracle if she could get outside that room,' grinned Cusher. 'We're keeping her tied up all the time, only releasing her hands and taking off the gag while she eats.'

'That's right,' said Mr. Hillbury approvingly. 'Be extra careful, George — extra careful.'

'How does she come into it?' asked Cusher. 'You never told me that.'

'And I don't intend to tell you,' said Mr. Hillbury softly. 'There are quite a lot of things I haven't told you, George, and that's one of them. Don't get curious, my friend. You're getting well paid for what you do and there's a lot to come for both you and Sam when this business is over. That should be sufficient.'

'Oh, I ain't grumbling,' replied Cusher quickly. 'I'm quite satisfied, only you're running a bit of a risk, that's all. If the police took it into their 'eads to search this 'ouse we should all be in the soup.'

'They would have to get a warrant before they could do that,' retorted the fat man, 'and I don't see that they have any grounds for applying for one. But even if they did and got in I don't think they'd find anything.'

He told the other of his plans concerning the old well, which he had previously mentioned to his wife.

Cusher looked at him admiringly.

'You're a cute 'n ain't yer, guv'nor,' said the man with a grin. 'I call that real clever.'

'I'm not entirely devoid of intelligence,' answered Mr. Hillbury, modestly. 'Is Mrs. Hillbury up yet?'

'I ain't seen 'er,' replied George, shaking his head.

Mr. Hillbury grunted and went on eating his egg.

Cusher lingered for a moment and then seeing that the other was occupied with his thoughts turned on his heel and left the room.

For an hour he sat, planning and scheming, and his meditations were eventually interrupted by the entrance of the woman. He scowled at her through a cloud of smoke.

'Oh, you've got up, have you,' he grunted. 'I thought you intended stopping in bed all day.'

'Supposing I had?' she retorted coolly. 'There's nothing very much to get up for, is there.' She pulled a chair up to the table, sat down and poured herself out some coffee, eyeing the man opposite to her with disfavour.

'You look a wreck,' she remarked. 'You never were at your best in the morning.'

'You don't look so good yourself,' he snarled, 'and if you can't say anything pleasant keep your mouth shut.'

'Could anybody look good, as you call it, in a place like this,' she grumbled. 'How much longer are we going to stay here, buried alive in the country? Might as well be in prison.'

'It's as bad for me, isn't it,' snapped her husband. 'D'you suppose I like it? D'you think I live here for amusement?' He pushed back his chair angrily and rose to his feet. 'I'm just as sick of it as you are, but it's safe.'

'Safe!' There was a world of contempt in her voice as she repeated the word.

'You were always a coward, weren't you! Scared to death of your own skin. Why don't you show a bit of pluck instead of hiding away like a rat in a hole — '

'You shut up and mind your own business.' He swung round on her, his fists clenched, and for a moment she thought he was going to strike her. 'I'm looking after this business and I'll look after it in my own way — see. If you don't like being here, clear out.'

'And leave you with the stuff,' she sneered. 'No, thank you, that doesn't appeal to little Myra. I'm sticking here until you go, unless you'd like to give me my share in advance.'

His momentary temper had subsided and he faced her coolly.

'It wouldn't do you any good if I did,' he said. 'You couldn't do anything with it, you know that. See here, Myra, it's no good you and I quarrelling. Being cooped up in this wretched place has got on our nerves, but I don't think we shall be here much longer.'

'That's the first piece of good news I've heard for months,' said the woman.

'What's the idea?'

'It's Cusher's really,' he answered, and told her. To his surprise she was disapproving.

'I don't like it,' she said, and her eyes were troubled. 'You've never gone in for killing before, Lew, although you've done most other things. I'd rather you dropped the idea, even if it meant staying here indefinitely.'

'If this fellow gets the chance he'll kill me,' answered Hillbury. 'There's no doubt about that, and while he's alive life isn't worth living. Once we get him out of the way, we are safe. We can leave this place and go abroad, with enough money to last us the rest of our lives.'

'And what about the girl?' she demanded. 'You couldn't take her with you, and you daren't release her.'

'I shouldn't dream of doing either,' he replied. 'She'd have to go the same way as her father.'

'Well, I'll have no hand in it,' said Mrs. Hillbury decisively. 'I've helped you in a lot of schemes, but I draw the line at murder. It was a fool trick bringing the girl here at all, I said so at the beginning.'

'It was the most sensible thing I ever did,' he retorted. 'Heaven knows what would have happened by now if we hadn't had her as a hostage.'

'That's all very well,' she said, extracting a cigarette from a tiny case and tapping it daintily on her finger nail 'But now you've got her you can't get rid of her without violence. She knows too much.'

'Isn't that what I've been saying,' he argued. 'My plan is the only way, and I'm going to do it.'

Before she could answer a bell shrilled insistently from somewhere outside the room.

'That's the telephone,' said Hillbury, looking at her a little startled. 'Who the devil can be ringing us up?'

'Perhaps it's the police,' she suggested, flicking open a little gold lighter and dipping the end of her cigarette in its flame

'Ah, yes, most likely,' he agreed, and going out of the room he crossed the hall to the little office-like apartment where he had interviewed Jim Brent and Laker on the previous night.

'Hello,' he called, and at the sound of the voice that came in answer over the wire his flabby face went grey.

'Is that you, Gleeson?' it said. 'Listen, you'd better watch out. I got one of your comic guards last night. Very soon now I'll be getting you.'

Shaking in every limb Mr. Hillbury tried to control his voice sufficiently to speak clearly.

'See here, Harry,' he quavered, 'why carry on this feud? Why not be sensible?'

The man at the other end of the wire gave a hard laugh.

'Sensible, eh?' he retorted. 'I think I'm being very sensible. It's no good trying any soft soap on me, Lew; I haven't got the forgive and forget spirit; there's nothing of turn the other cheek about me. You've shut yourself up in a house like a prison and surrounded yourself with broken-down pugilists but you can't keep me away from you. I can get into your house just whenever I please. Get that.'

Mr. Hillbury got it, and almost dropped the receiver in his terror.

'Why bear malice, Harry?' he said. 'Why not come and see me and chat the matter over in a friendly way? After all, there's enough for both of us — '

'You never were clever, Lew,' broke in the other. 'I suppose you think I can't see through your idea. Walk into my parlour said the spider to the fly, eh? No, thank you. I'll come and see you at my own time and when you least expect me. You should have thought of all that 'being enough for both of us' stuff before. You were greedy, and you've got to pay for your greediness.'

'I'm sorry you won't listen to reason,' said Mr. Hillbury keeping his voice steady by an effort. 'It might have saved a lot of trouble. I wouldn't like any harm to come to your daughter.'

'No harm will come to her,' snapped the voice. 'You'll see to that for the sake of your fat hide. I'm going to kill you, anyway, but if you've harmed a hair of Lesley's head when I find her you will welcome death as an end to your misery. I'll make that fat body of yours squirm in agony.'

'Don't you think it's rather dangerous to utter threats like that?' said the fat man, though his forehead was damp with the perspiration that had suddenly broken out on it.

'You try anything and see,' replied the other harshly. 'And remember, Gleeson, I'm close to you all the time. I'm not going to tell you when I'm coming for you, because I rather think the uncertainty will give you many unpleasant moments.'

There was a click as the receiver was hung up, and Mr. Hillbury staggered away from his own telephone shaking in every limb, his face the colour of chalk. The man who had just spoken had not threatened idly, none knew that better than he. He would have to redouble his precautious, be on his guard night and day.

He came out of the little room unsteadily and his face was the face of a man who has heard his death sentence.

11

Perfecto Virginias

Both Freddy Kemp and Phyllis Orde were inclined to be a little sceptical concerning Jim's assertion that he had seen someone looking at them from the upstairs window of Lady's Manor.

'Most probably it was a trick of the light, old boy,' said the journalist, 'and your mind being full of the queer faced fellow, imagined the rest. I didn't see anything.'

'Neither did I,' said the girl, shaking her head.

Jim refrained from arguing the point. He knew he had not been mistaken all the same. For the fraction of a second, that face he had seen in the wood had looked out at him from behind the dirty glass of the window, and then, as though its owner had become suddenly aware that he might be seen, it had vanished.

It was no trick of the light. Apart from the black servant and the man they had just interviewed, there was a third person in Lady's Manor — the man who had killed his father and the murderer of Dan Killick.

They drove back to the inn, and after lunch, Jim excused himself and going to his room wrote a long letter to Chief-Inspector Mason. It ran into several pages, and when he had completed it he read it through, enclosed it in an envelope and walked down to the post office to get a stamp. When he had slipped the letter into the box he strolled on towards the police station.

Superintendent Laker, the desk sergeant informed him, was in conference with the Chief Constable, and the awe in his voice suggested that this personage was not to be disturbed lightly.

He watched Jim with horrified eyes as, not in the least overwhelmed by the enormity of what he was doing, the young Inspector walked over to the little office and tapped on the door.

Laker was in his usual place behind his

desk and standing on the hearthrug in front of the tiny fireplace was a stoutish man, very neatly dressed, very red of face, whose rather prominent, pale blue eyes stared fiercely at the newcomer as he entered.

'Oh, come in, Mr. Brent,' said the Superintendent, quite unnecessarily, as Jim was already in.

He introduced the stout little man as Colonel Lucas.

'How do you do, sir?' said Jim pleasantly, and in reply the Colonel said, 'Huh!' and twisted his neatly waxed moustache with a puffy purplish hand.

In spite of the fact that he was dressed in Harris tweeds, Jim could almost hear the clinking of spurs, and had a feeling that he might be ordered to stand to attention at any moment.

'We've just been discussing this affair at Dead Trees,' said Laker. 'Haven't we, sir?'

Colonel Lucas said 'Huh!' again, and transferred his hand to the other side of his moustache.

'I've just been telling the Chief Constable how you came into it, Mr.

Brent,' continued the Superintendent, 'and he is of the opinion that we ought to apply for a search warrant.'

'Only thing to do,' grunted the Chief Constable, straddling his legs and clasping his hands behind his back. 'Find out for certain whether this gal's there or not, eh, what?'

'I agree with you, sir,' said Jim. 'In fact I was going to make the same suggestion.'

Another 'Huh!' came from the Colonel's lips.

'The events of last night are sufficient to prove that there's something fishy about Hillbury,' Jim went on, 'and if he has got a girl imprisoned at Dead Trees and we can find her she may be able to supply valuable evidence.'

'Seems incredible these days,' barked the Chief Constable, 'gal shut up and all that, but you never can tell. I remember when I was in command of the Brigade at Poona — '

They listened politely while he launched into a disjointed narrative about an English girl and a native chief. It was not very exciting, and when it came to an end Laker suppressed a yawn and came back to the business in hand.

'Well, then, if that's agreed upon,' he said, 'I'll go up and see Mr. Venning and get a search warrant signed. Mr. Venning,' he added for Jim's edification, 'is our local magistrate and Justice of the Peace.'

'When do you propose executing it?' enquired Jim.

'What about tomorrow morning?' answered the Superintendent, and Jim nodded. 'You'll come with us, of course.'

'I wouldn't miss it for the world,' replied Jim truthfully.

'Like to come myself,' grunted Colonel Lucas, 'but afraid I can't manage it. Don't get much excitement here, Mr. Brent. Pretty dull life for an old campaigner. When I was with the Brigade in India — '

'I expect you had some exciting times, sir,' said Jim hastily, fearing another long anecdote of the Colonel's adventures. 'Now there are one or two things I would like to discuss if you have the time.'

They discussed the situation and the line their further investigating were going

117

to take, the Chief Constable contributing an occasional 'Huh!' to the proceedings. His suggestion that a search warrant should be applied for in order to discover if there was any truth in the messages which had been flung over the wall of Dead Tress and which had first brought Jim into the affair, had apparently exhausted all his ideas on the subject.

'There's no doubt,' said Jim, 'that this man, Hillbury, is scared to death of the person who killed Killick. When I repeated the dead man's last words I've never seen anyone so frightened before in my life; he was the picture of terror.'

'I wonder what the fellow meant by 'Queer Face',' muttered Laker. 'It's a peculiar name to give anybody.'

Jim could have told him, but it was one of the things he wanted to follow up on his own, and he refrained. Laker was a good fellow but obviously hidebound by routine. He was also, although he hadn't attempted to assert his authority, Jim's superior officer. Not only would he undoubtedly look askance at the young Inspector's unauthorised intrusion into the grounds of Dead Trees,, but would probably take some steps that might result in the man slipping through their fingers altogether, and Jim had waited for this opportunity too long to risk anything like that happening. The unknown jewel thief who had killed his father had proved himself to be a man of cleverness and resource, his only mistake had been when he had walked into that trap set for him by old John Brent on the Rissac's lawn and he had got out of that in a way that showed him to be dangerous as well. Driven into a corner it was quite possible he would repeat his tactics and vanish once more into the unknown from whence he had come, and in that event there might never be an opportunity of finding him again. He had succeeded before in evading the police of the entire country for over three years and it was quite possible if he escaped this time he might do so for ever. So Jim kept his knowledge to himself and Superintendent Laker's question remained unanswered.

The Chief Constable took his departure shortly after, leaving the two of them alone, and when he had gone Laker heaved a sigh of relief.

'He's a little trying. Mr. Brent,' he said rather apologetically. 'Not a bad fellow really but has a theory that the police force should be run on army lines.'

'In short, like the brigade in Poona,' broke in Jim with a smile, and Laker nodded.

'That's it exactly,' he answered. 'Did you see Dr. Patterson-Willis, Mr. Brent?'

'Yes,' replied Jim. 'We saw him. An interesting man but rather abrupt in his manner.'

'I've never met him,' said Laker. 'I've seen him twice, I think, in the village but I've never spoken to him.'

'I shouldn't like to live in that house of his,' said Jim. 'It's in a very bad state of repair and has a most unpleasantly, creepy atmosphere about it.'

The Superintendent smiled. He was still intensely curious to know why Jim had elected to pay that visit to Lady's Manor but a certain reticence prevented him asking the question direct.

'It's a very old place, you know,' he

replied. 'I think I told you that, and I suppose it suits his purpose since he's so seldom in residence.'

'Who looks after it while he's away?' asked Jim.

'Nobody,' answered Laker. 'It's shut up.'

'So the black servant comes and goes with his master,' said the young Inspector, and Laker's long face looked surprised.

'Black servant.' he repeated. 'That's a new one on me. Has he got a black servant now? He used to employ an ex-serviceman — a man named Colley. I knew him' — he smiled reminiscently, 'because I had a little trouble with him once. The doctor went up to town for the weekend and Colley thought, it was a good opportunity to have a fling. He was only a little chap, but knocked out three men before they threw him out of the Cricketer's Arms — that's the pub on the green — and it took two constables to bring him to the station.'

'If he went on like that often,' said Jim, 'I'm not surprised Patterson-Willis got rid of him.'

'He didn't,' said Laker, 'he was quite a sober fellow as a rule. He liked his drink but that was the first time I ever saw him drunk. He used to do all the shopping and was rather a favourite in the village, particularly with Mrs. Meaker's daughter who keeps the tobacconist's. They used to get special cigarettes for him — he didn't smoke 'em but the doctor did. Perfecto Hand Made Virginias, at eight shillings a hundred.'

Jim's face was expressionless, but his brain was working rapidly, Perfecto Hand Made Virginias was the same brand as the cigarette-end that he had picked up in the wood.

12

The Shadow on the Blind

When Jim left the little station house he decided to go for a walk before returning to the inn. He had much to think about and hoped that the exercise would help to clarify his thoughts.

The afternoon was hot and sultry, even warmer if anything than the day before, and turning off the High Street he chose a shady lane that wound through the woods up the hillside.

The fact that he had just learned that Dr. Patterson-Willis was a smoker of Perfecto Virginias strengthened his conviction that there was a connection between the specialist on skin diseases and the man with the queer face. On the face of it, it seemed incredible that a well-known personage like Patterson-Willis could be mixed up in any way with the unknown jewel robber and murderer, but Jim in his short experience had come across many things that were even less credible and had proved the truth. Patterson-Willis like so many men might not be all that he seemed. It was quite possible that there was another side to his character, a less pleasant side, which up to now he had succeeded in hiding from the world in general. There might be some secret in his life which this man had become aware of and which he was using to force the doctor to do his bidding. Again Patterson-Willis might be a completely innocent agent, it was possible that 'Queer Face' had contracted some disease like leprosy or allied to leprosy, which interested the doctor from a professional point of view. He might be staying at Lady's Manor in the capacity of a patient, in which case Willis would quite naturally keep his presence a secret and his excursions at night could be undertaken without the doctor's knowledge.

He was so occupied with his thoughts that he walked further than he intended and it was nearly six o'clock when he got back to the inn. He found Freddy Kemp consuming beer in the bar and accepted the large man's cheery invitation to join him with alacrity.

'Where's Miss Orde?' he asked presently, removing his nose from the cool interior of the tankard.

'Gone to inspect her digs,' said Freddy. 'They only had one extra room here besides yours, and the landlady recommended Phil to a friend of hers who lives in a cottage a little way away.'

'And I take it that you have grabbed the vacant room here,' said Jim, signalling to the barman to refill the empty tankards.

'Correct, O Chief,' said Freddy, 'and now I have a small item of news for you. I got on to the *Clarion* this afternoon, and told them about my failure to get the interview with Patterson-Willis, and they were most surprised. They were under the impression that everything had been fixed up. When they 'phoned Willis yesterday morning he was only too eager, absolutely jumped at the idea, terms were arranged and everything. Now, what do you think of that?'

'The only thing to be made of it,' said

Jim, 'is that between then and the time we saw him he changed his mind.'

'Marvellous!' said Freddy in mock admiration. 'Famous detective shows colossal powers of deduction!'

'Don't be an ass,' said Jim, 'if you can help it.'

'Well, we know he changed his mind,' retorted his friend. 'What I want to know is why did he change his mind?'

Jim shrugged his shoulders.

'Ask me something easier,' he answered, and curiously enough the very simple and obvious answer never occurred to him.

'All the same, there is something peculiar about Patterson-Willis,' he continued. 'Do you remember my telling you about the cigarette end I picked up in the wood?'

Freddy removed the tankard from his lips and nodded.

'Well, Willis smokes the same brand,' said Jim.

He told the journalist what he had heard from Laker that afternoon.

'It certainly looks,' commented Freddy Kemp, 'as if Willis would bear further investigation.'

'That's what I think,' agreed Jim, 'and I propose to do little preliminary work in that direction tonight.'

The bar was empty and they had kept their voices low, but now with a glance round Jim lowered his voice still further.

'I think a visit to Lady's Manor after dark would be interesting,' he said. 'I know you thought I was letting my imagination run away with me when I told you I saw somebody at that window over the porch, but I'm sure I did, and I'm sure it was the same fellow I saw in the wood. If I'm right he's a night bird, and if he contemplates any activity tonight I think it would be a good idea to be on the spot.'

'I'm with you,' said the journalist, his eyes sparkling. 'That is if you want me to be in it.'

'Of course I want you to be in it,' said Jim, 'that's why I told you.' He finished the remains of his beer and set down the empty tankard.

'Come along to my room,' he said, 'and we'll discuss the plan of campaign.'

* * *

It was a perfect night with not a cloud to mar the blue serenity of the sky when they left the Load of Hay by way of Jim's window and the lean-to shed as he had done on the previous night. Not a light shone in any of the little cottages and houses as they walked up the High Street, and there was no evidence of life whatever until breasting the slope that led up to the gates of Dead Trees an owl hooted somewhere in the woods to their right.

It was difficult going for the surface was bad and full of unexpected ruts, but they managed it without any casualties and eventually found themselves near the iron gates which gave admittance to the drive.

They had previously decided not to use this means of ingress for it was quite likely that there might be some attachment to the gate which would warn the inhabitants of the house of their approach. Jim had decided that a far better plan would be to scale the low stone wall that surrounded the grounds.

They set off on a voyage of exploration to find a suitable point. They walked on, the lane growing narrower and narrower as they proceeded. After about a hundred yards it took a sharp turn to the right following the direction of the wall. Here the track was so narrow that they had to walk in single file. The trees of the wood on the left grew closer in.

'I think this will do,' whispered Jim, his lips close to Kemp's ear, and they halted.

To drop from the wall to the ground beyond was easy, and presently they found themselves standing knee deep in undergrowth and surrounded by darkness that was so impenetrable that it almost seemed solid.

After a moment or two, they began to move forward in the direction of the house. Their progress was necessarily slow for the undergrowth hampered their movements. Trailing vines clung round their ankles and had to be carefully disengaged for it was essential that they should make as little noise as possible. It seemed to Jim that they were hours groping their way through thickly growing bushes before they came out into a clearing where the ground was free of brambles and walking was easier. It was also lighter here for they had emerged from the shadow of the trees and across a neglected patch of garden they saw the low bulk of the house, flanked by a screen of trees which stood out sharply black against the deep blue of the sky.

Looking about him he discovered that the belt of shrubbery through which they had fought their way extended in a semi-circle almost up to the house, where it was lost in the dense shadows. So long as they kept in the cover of this it would take a very keen eye indeed to detect their presence, and he confided this plan in a whisper to Freddy Kemp. The journalist nodded in agreement.

With Jim leading and Freddy following they began to make their way along the border of the shrubbery, hugging the closely growing bushes and keeping in the shadow of their overhanging branches. The shrubbery ended at a narrow path that was an extension of the drive and apparently encircled the house. The great, black branches of the cypress tree gave the whole place a very eerie and sinister aspect. It had been bad enough in the daylight when the sun was shining, but now, in the darkness of the night, that atmosphere of stillness and stealthiness, of some brooding terror, was increased a thousandfold.

They followed the path round past the dilapidated out-buildings to the back of the house, and here Jim stopped so suddenly that Freddy Kemp, who had not been prepared for the manoeuvre, almost fell over him.

'Blast!' said the big journalist as his nose came into contact with Jim's head.

'Shut up,' said the young Inspector. 'Look there!'

Rubbing his nose tenderly Freddy followed the direction of his hand. From one of the upstairs windows a light was shining.

Signing to the journalist to follow him, Jim advanced cautiously until they were in a line with the window. Judging from its position it appeared to be the window of one of the bedrooms, but of that they could not be certain for the blind was drawn and it was impossible to see into the rooms. Even if the blind has been up they would only have been able to see a portion of the ceiling from where they were standing, but there was a clump of trees nearby and it occurred to Jim that by climbing one of these — had the blind not intervened — it would have been possible to have got a clear view into the room. However, the steadily burning light denoted one thing, somebody was still wakeful in Lady Manor.

He looked at the luminous dial of his wristwatch and saw that it was ten minutes past one and as he raised his eyes again, a shadow passed behind the blind.

It was the shadow of a man. Tall and thin. Blurred and distorted it crossed the white screen and disappeared leaving a blank, only to return after the lapse of a few seconds and re-cross in the opposite direction. This time the shadow was more distinct; the man had come nearer to the window and was more sharply silhouetted. It was not the shadow of the black servant and it was certainly not the shadow of Dr. Patterson-Willis. There was a third inhabitant of Lady's Manor, and it could only be the queer-faced man whom Jim had seen momentarily staring at him through the window of the room above the porch.

13

The Search

Jim yawned, opened his eyes and blinked at the bright sunlight streaming into his bedroom. Through the mists of sleep that still blurred his senses he heard a vague knocking on his door and grunted an invitation to the knocker to come in. Joyce, the smiling faced girl who waited on them at the Load of Hay, entered, carrying his morning tea.

'Good morning, sir,' she said as she set this down on the little table by his bedside. 'It's a beautiful day.'

Jim struggled up into a sitting position and rubbed his eyes. 'What's the time?' he asked.

'A quarter past eight, sir,' answered the girl. 'I'm a little late this morning.'

She went out, closing the door behind her, and sipping his tea Jim looked out of the window.

He was feeling desperately tired for it had been after four when he and Freddy Kemp had got back from their midnight excursion, and except for the proof that there was a third person at Lady's Manor they had received little reward for their lack of sleep.

For half an hour the unknown man had paced up and down in the lighted room and then the light had been extinguished, and although Jim and the journalist had kept watch until the small hours of the morning, until indeed dawn was well advanced, there had been no other sign or sound of life in the house. The young Inspector had hoped that this wakefulness on the part of one of the inhabitants had presaged a nocturnal excursion, but nothing of the sort had taken place. Nobody had attempted to leave Lady's Manor that night, and eventually they had returned to the inn, disappointed and almost dead from fatigue.

Jim swallowed his tea and feeling more or less wakeful jumped out of bed and began his morning toilet. The Load of Hay was not sufficiently modern to possess a bathroom so he had to make do with a cold wash down in the basin. His shaving water had been left outside his door, and when he had shaved and dressed, he went down to the coffee room. There was no sign of Freddy Kemp, and he learnt from Joyce, who was laying the table for breakfast, that the big journalist had refused his tea and given orders that he was not to be disturbed. Jim smiled, and ate his meal in solitary state.

After he had finished it and smoked a pipe in the gaily hung garden, he left word that he would meet Kemp for lunch and went down to the police station.

Superintendent Laker had already arrived and was standing talking to the desk sergeant in the charge room.

'Good morning, Mr. Brent,' he greeted. 'I've got the warrant all signed and fixed and as soon as Sergeant Lumley arrives we'll go along up to Dead Trees.'

Sergeant Lumley arrived just as he'd finished speaking. He was a pleasant faced man whose round cheeks glowed with health, and his uniform seemed to be at least two sizes too small for him.

'Very pleased to meet you, sir,' he said smilingly when Laker introduced them. 'So you're coming with us this morning, eh?'

It was more of a statement than a question and since it obviously required no answer Jim made none, and apparently Sergeant Lumley expected no reply for he turned almost at once to Laker.

'Miller's gone round to get the car, Super,' he said. 'It will be here in a few minutes.'

It was exactly three minutes later when the car arrived and going out to it, Jim and the Superintendent got in the back, while the sergeant took his place beside the constable at the wheel.

The heavy wooden gates of Dead Trees, which made the place look more like a factory than the entrance to a private residence, were closed as usual when the constable brought the car to a halt opposite them, and Jim wondered as they got out, what the result of this search would be. Would they find the girl whose message had been the means of bringing him into this extraordinary business, or had Mr. Hillbury taken the precaution of spiriting her away to some safer hiding place? That the message had been genuine he had no doubt.

Superintendent Laker pressed the bell and waited. He waited even longer than he had done on that previous occasion when he and Jim had come to demand an explanation of the scrawled appeal, which had been thrown over the wall. He waited so long that he got impatient and rang the bell again, but he had scarcely removed his finger from the button when the slit-like letterbox was jerked open, and Cusher's voice demanded to know what they wanted.

'We wish to see Mr. Hillbury,' said Laker curtly,

'He ain't up yet,' answered Cusher. 'Can't you come back later?'

'No we can't,' snapped the Superintendent. 'You just go and tell your master that we want to see him, and look sharp about it, my man.'

Cusher growled something below his breath and the flap clicked shut. They heard his retreating footsteps fade away on the gravel of the drive and settled down to await his return. He was a very long time, but when he did come back he made no demur about admitting them, even offered an apology for his tardiness.

'I'm sorry,' he said ungraciously as he opened the gate, 'but Mr. Hillbury took a lot of waking. Come in, will you?'

They crossed the threshold and Cusher shut and relocked the wicket behind them.

Mr. Hillbury was standing in the hall when they entered, his flabby face an unhealthy grey and patches of perspiration standing out on his forehead. He was dressed in a dressing gown, which he had hastily assumed over a pair of pyjamas, and what little hair he possessed was dishevelled.

'This is a very early call, Superintendent,' he greeted and looked sharply at Jim and the sergeant. 'What can I do for you?'

'I have a warrant to search this house, sir,' answered Laker without preliminary, and the fat man started.

'A warrant?' he repeated. 'To search my house? But this is outrageous. I shall certainly not permit any such thing.'

'I'm afraid you have no choice, sir,' said Laker quietly. 'The warrant is quite in order and I must insist that you offer no opposition to our carrying it out.'

'I suppose it's useless arguing,' he grunted. 'If you wish to waste your time searching people's houses you must do so. Where do you want to begin?'

'We'll begin with the ground floor, if you please, sir,' said Laker in a business-like tone. 'I shall be glad if you will produce any keys that may assist us.'

'The keys are upstairs in my room,' said the fat man. 'Get them, will you, Cusher?'

The ugly-faced servant who had been standing sullenly by nodded, and began to ascend the staircase. While they were waiting for him to return the Superintendent took a blue paper from his pocket and gave it to Hillbury.

'You may as well have this now, sir,' he said. 'It's the subpoena to attend the inquest tomorrow morning on your servant, Dan Killick.'

Mr. Hillbury took it, glanced at it and thrust it into the pocket of his dressing gown.

'I don't know what you expect to find at this house,' he said, 'but apparently you're within your rights searching it. I must, however, warn you that I shall make a very strong complaint to your superiors.'

'Regarding that, you must do as you think best, sir,' replied the Superintendent calmly, and at that moment Cusher returned with the keys.

They began with the ground floor and the cellars, but they found nothing. Neither did the rooms on the second and third floor reveal anything of a suspicious character. Sergeant Lumley was the first to make any discovery at all, but that turned out to be very meagre. He had left Jim and Laker to examine the third floor and gone higher up, and presently he called to them over the banisters.

'Will you come up here a minute, Super,' he said. 'I've found something that looks rummy.'

Laker went up followed by Jim, and found the sergeant standing outside the open door of a room, the walls of which were completely padded with leather, the light being admitted from a skylight in the roof.

'What was this used for?' asked the Superintendent, turning to Mr. Hillbury, who had accompanied them on their search.

The fat man shook his head.

'I never used it at all,' he said. 'I daresay you know this house was once used as an asylum? Anyway the room was there when I took it, and I've always kept it locked.'

Jim crossed the threshold of the strange apartment, and as he did so he sniffed. A faint whiff of perfume came to his nostrils — the same perfume he had smelt in the hall the day they had first visited Dead Trees.

'You're sure there hasn't been a woman here recently?' he asked sharply, but Mr. Hillbury, who had been watching him closely, and guessed the reason for that sniff, was ready with an explanation.

'You mean the scent,' he said calmly. 'I smelt that when I first took over the house. It was stronger then; probably the last patient who was shut up in that horrible place used it. It would naturally cling to the leather.'

It was a plausible explanation, and Jim admired the man's quick brain for having thought of it.

He saw something on the rubber floor, and, stooping, picked it up. It was a crumb of bread, and when he crumbled it in his fingers he found it was fresh.

'I suppose that's a relic of the last patient, too,' he remarked.

'Probably,' replied Hillbury coolly. 'Anyhow, I know nothing about it.'

There was nothing else in the room, and Jim turned reluctantly away. They had examined the whole house now excepting the roof, and when this had been inspected they were forced to the conclusion that there was no sign of the girl who had signed herself Lesley Allerton.

'Well, have you found what you expected?' sneered Mr. Hillbury as they descended to the hall.

'You know very well we haven't,' answered Jim, 'but we haven't quite finished yet. We've still got the grounds to examine.'

For a moment he detected a flicker of uneasiness in the man's eyes. It was gone almost immediately, but he wondered.

The grounds took a long time, for they were extensive, but they diligently explored every inch of them, including a dilapidated greenhouse and some mouldering outbuildings that had once been stables.

'I'm afraid we've struck a mare's-nest, Mr. Brent,' said Laker disappointedly when they had finished. 'If there ever was a girl here they've succeeded in getting her away.'

'And there was a girl here, I'm willing to bet anything on that,' replied Jim. 'That fat brute in there has been too clever for us, that's all.'

Mr. Hillbury was waiting for them at the foot of the steps as they came back to the house, and his flabby face was creased into a smile of satisfaction. 'Well,' he remarked, rubbing his flabby hands, 'have you found anything? Have you discovered the stolen jewels or the beautiful heroine gagged and bound, or maybe a cache of noxious drugs?' He shook his head slowly. 'I'm afraid, Superintendent, you've been reading too many sensational novels.'

'I'll admit,' said Jim, 'that the last words of your servant, Dan Killick, was like something out of a sensational novel.'

The smile left the fat man's face abruptly.

'It's my opinion he was delirious,' he said sharply. 'He couldn't have meant anything.'

'You don't know anybody who answers that description 'Queer Face'?' said Jim.

'No, I don't!' snarled the fat man, but Jim saw the fear in his eyes and felt that the morning had not been entirely wasted.

14

The Girl Who Vanished

Mr. Hillbury stood watching the departing figures of Jim and the two police officers and the expression on his unpleasant face was triumphant. They would have to get up very early in the morning to catch him, he thought, and chuckled softly.

The tone of the Superintendent's message had shown that was not a friendly visit, and they had had to work quickly. Sam had gone out for a little exercise, and he and Cusher had had to do the job between them. It had been difficult work getting the girl downstairs, for his muscles were flaccid with long disuse and she was by no means a light weight. Time, too, had been a consideration. It was not policy to keep their visitors waiting too long, it might, have aroused needless suspicion. Anyway they had succeeded, and the girl, gagged and bound, had been lowered safely into the well at the end of a rope, the cover shut down and covered with earth so that there was nothing to distinguish its presence.

Mr. Hillbury stood blinking and smiling to himself in the sunlight, and looked rather like an overfed tabby cat that had just finished a meal off a particularly plump bird. He watched his recent visitors disappear round the bend of the drive and then, turning, re-entered the house.

His wife was lounging in a chair in the drawing room, a position she had occupied all through the search, and she raised her eyes as he came in and helped himself to a cigarette from the box on the table.

'Well?' she inquired.

'Quite well,' he answered complacently. 'They've gone.'

'Yes, they've gone,' he repeated. 'And I don't think they'll come back. I shall most certainly lodge a complaint with the Chief Constable.'

'D'you think that's wise?' she murmured.

'Of course,' said her husband. 'It's the natural thing to do. If I don't do it, it will look suspicious.'

'I don't think that man Brent was satisfied,' she said, and the fat man snapped his fingers.

'Oh, him!' he said contemptuously and ungrammatically. 'I don't care whether he was satisfied or not. He can't do anything, and that's all that matters.'

'I wouldn't be too sure of that,' said the woman warningly, and Mr. Hillbury frowned.

'What do you mean?' he snapped. 'What can he do? They've searched the house and they haven't found what they expected. It's very doubtful if they'll institute a second search — but even if they do it will have the same result. Brent may be as suspicious as he damn well pleases, but he can't prove anything.'

'Well, I shouldn't be too confident if I were you,' she said, and then, changing the subject abruptly: 'Hadn't you better go and fetch the girl back?'

He nodded.

'Yes, I will, as soon as Cusher returns,' he replied. 'There's no hurry, she's quite all right where she is.'

'The air in these old wells isn't too good sometimes,' she remarked. 'It's just as well — '

'You needn't worry about that,' he broke in, 'I tested that some time ago, when the idea first occurred to me. Cusher and I lowered a candle on the end of a string and the air was sweet enough. By the way, I've got to go to the inquest on Killick tomorrow, which isn't too pleasant.'

'You've got to go,' she said. 'You'd better be careful, Lew — '

'Oh, they've got nothing on me!' he interrupted. 'I didn't kill the fellow.'

'I'm not thinking of the police,' she retorted. 'I'm thinking of — him.'

His air of assurance dropped from him and his face changed.

'He — he can't do anything in broad daylight,' he muttered. 'What do you think he can do?'

'There are lots of things he can do,'

answered his wife. 'A shot from the wood opposite the gate as you come out, or perhaps on that lonely bit of road leading down to the village. It would be easy. Just as easy by daylight as any other time.'

An ugly pallor spread over Mr. Hillbury's face.

'Yes, you are right,' he said huskily. 'I shall have to be careful. I'd better have a car sent up; the big gates can be opened and it can come right up to the house and fetch me.'

His hand shook as he drew jerkily at his cigarette.

'My God! I wish it was as easy to tackle Harry as it was the police this morning,' he muttered, 'but he's too clever, and cunning as a monkey, always was.'

'You were a fool not to play straight with him,' said the woman; 'then we shouldn't have had to live in this constant atmosphere of fear.'

He swung round on her, his teeth bared in a snarl.

'What's the good of talking like that now,' he snapped angrily, 'How was I to know that he'd ever come back? I thought

150

he was finished. I never thought he'd recover, and you were just as keen as I was to grab the lot.'

'Perhaps I was at the time,' she replied, helping herself to a cigarette, 'but I didn't know then what we were letting ourselves in for. Why don't you offer to give the stuff up and be done with it. Without it we shouldn't be penniless, and you can easily make more money.'

'I have,' he said irritably. 'He rang me up — I didn't tell you — but he rang me up, and I asked him to come and chat the whole thing over, offered to give him the stuff, but he wouldn't hear of it. He's mad. He's only got one idea in his head, and that's to get back on me for double-crossing him. He wouldn't listen to reason, just laughed at me.'

He flung his half-smoked cigarette into the fender, and, taking a handkerchief from his dressing gown, wiped his moist face.

'I don't know,' began the woman, and stopped as he shot her a warning glance.

'Be careful,' he muttered, 'George is coming back.'

Cusher's footsteps clattered across the hall, and a second later he appeared in the doorway.

'Well, they've 'opped it,' he said with a grin, 'and they don't look none too pleased with themselves either.'

'That'll worry me a lot,' grunted Mr. Hillbury. 'We'd better go and get the girl back now; come and give me a hand, George.'

He went out with Cusher at his heels, and going round to a shed at the back of the house, armed himself with a spade.

With this implement tucked under his arm he made his way towards a belt of shrubbery in a shady and neglected portion of the garden. Forcing his way through the bushes, he came out in a clearing in the centre and began to shovel away the earth until a circular cover of decayed and rotten wood was revealed. In the middle was a rusty iron ring, and when he had completely cleared away the mould, which had covered it, he signed to Cusher. Stooping, the man grasped the ring, and after a little effort succeeded in moving the heavy lid.

It had been resting on the circular brick coping of an old well. A current of cold air came up from the dark shaft as Mr. Hillbury bent over and felt for the staple that had been driven into the moss-covered side.

'You'd better take the weight,' he grunted, 'while I untie the knot.'

Cusher nodded, and stretching himself full length grasped the rope that vanished into the black depths. The next second he gave a startled exclamation.

'By Gosh, guv'nor, there ain't no weight!'

'No weight!' snapped Mr. Hillbury. 'What — '

'The rope's hanging loose,' broke in Cusher, 'there ain't nothin' on the end of it.'

To prove his words he pulled with one hand and the rope came up easily.

'It must have broken,' grunted Mr. Hillbury. 'Pull it up quickly.'

His voice shook a little as he peered horrified into the well. Cusher pulled in the slack rope, hand over hand, and presently, as the end came in sight, the fat man leaned forward and seized it eagerly.

'My God!' he said in a low voice. 'It hasn't broken, it's been cut!'

'Cut!' Cusher glared at the rope in his hand as if it had been a live snake. 'It can't have been cut, guv'nor.'

'Well, look at it,' said Mr. Hillbury. 'There are no frayed edges.'

'It must have been a faulty piece,' muttered Cusher frowning. 'It looks as if it had been cut, but it couldn't have been — it's impossible.'

'Well, if it broke,' said the fat man impatiently, 'the girl must be down there somewhere. Go and get a candle and some string. Luckily there's no water.'

The man hurried away, and Mr. Hillbury stood staring fearfully, first at the rope in his hand and then into the blackness of the well shaft. There was no water, the well had long since dried up, but if the rope had broken the girl must have had a nasty fall, perhaps a fatal fall. He shivered, and glanced uneasily about him. It was no part of his plan that she should die — at least not yet, not until he was assured that he had nothing to fear from his terrible enemy. An echo of that hard voice that had spoken to him over the telephone rang in his ears.

'I'm going to kill you anyway, but if you've harmed a hair of Lesley's head when I find her you will welcome death as an end to your misery. I'll make that fat body of yours squirm in agony.'

Mr. Hillbury's fat body squirmed at that moment, and the perspiration started out on his forehead. The girl couldn't be dead. She might be badly bruised, but nothing more serious. The question was, how were they going to get her up? Sam or Cusher would have to go down at the end of a rope, that was the only way. But supposing she was dead? The possibility sent him almost into a panic, and by the time Cusher returned with the candle and string he was shaking with the terror his imagination had conjured up.

The candle was fixed to a piece of wire, and the string tied round a loop in this, and when the wick had been lighted Cusher lowered it slowly into the well. The yellow flame grew dimmer as it descended, a flickering splash of light in the circular column of blackness, but it was a sufficiently powerful illumination to light up a yard or two of the shaft in its immediate vicinity. Down, down it went, and Mr. Hillbury followed its course eagerly.

'Touched bottom,' grunted Cusher at last, and leaning over the edge, they both peered at the feeble glimmer so far below, the fat man fearfully, wondering what it might reveal. But it revealed nothing.

The well was not very deep, and they could plainly see the rubble-strewn bottom, and nothing else. No huddled body showed up in the light of the candle. Nothing. Lesley Allerton had completely disappeared.

15

Cheese Day on Wednesday

Over lunch at the Load of Hay Jim told Freddy Kemp of the fiasco of the morning. 'H'm,' commented the big journalist with a grin. 'Almost as bad as our nocturnal excursion to Lady's Manor.'

'Worse,' retorted Jim. 'At least we learned something from that.' He reached for the mustard and then went on: 'I'm rather worried about what's become of that girl, Freddy. I wish I knew what had happened to her.'

He did not know it at the time, but he was echoing the fervent wish of Mr. Hillbury.

'They must have been pretty quick in getting her out of the way,' said Freddy, speaking with difficulty, his mouth full of cold chicken. 'That is, of course,' he added, 'if she was ever there.'

'I'm sure she was there,' said Jim, 'and

I'm sure she was confined in that room — the padded room I was telling you about. Apart from the scent, that crumb I picked up was fresh. It hadn't been there more than a few hours at the outside, and fresh breadcrumbs don't get into a locked room without a reason.'

'Well,' said the journalist, having washed down the chicken with a long draught of beer, 'she isn't there any longer, and it strikes me that you're going to have the dickens of a difficulty in finding her, unless you can make Hillbury squeal. You don't know where she is, who she is, what she looks like or anything about her.'

'That's true,' said Jim, and frowned.

Freddy Kemp, watching his gloomy face and guessing the reason, said nothing. He understood exactly what was passing in his friend's mind and sympathised, but it was difficult to offer anything in the nature of practical consolation so he took refuge in silence.

When luncheon was over Kemp rose to his feet and stretched himself with a yawn. 'I don't know what you're going to do,' he said, 'but I'm going for a walk with Phil.'

'I'll come with you,' replied Jim promptly, 'unless it's a case of two's company.'

'Don't be an ass,' growled the journalist. 'You know perfectly well there's nothing between Phil and me except friendship, although if rumour had its way we should have been married long ago and the possessors of a large and increasing family. Come on, a brisk walk will do you good.'

They paused to buy some cigarettes at the bar, and leaving the inn made their way in the direction of the pretty little cottage in which Phyllis Orde had taken up her quarters. The girl was waiting for them at the gate and they set off in the direction of the tree-clad hills, which looked as though they might offer a pleasant oasis of shade from the shimmering heat of the afternoon.

The weather still remained glorious although there was evidence that a break might be expected. On the previous day and during the morning the sky had been cloudless, but now little drifts were beginning to pile up on the horizon. Thick woolly clouds that hinted at a storm. There was not a breath of wind anywhere; the leaves on the trees hung limp and motionless and the whole countryside lay grilling in the scorching sun. Distant objects showed up sharp and clear in the overheated air and seemed to be nearer than they really were.

Twenty minutes' walk brought them to the fringe of the wooded slope, which had been their objective, and following a little twisting footpath that led upwards through the trees they penetrated deeper into the cool green shadiness of the wood.

'Gosh, but that's a relief!' grunted Freddy Kemp, pulling out his handkerchief and mopping his large and streaming face. 'Crossing that field has made me feel like a piece of grilled steak.'

'And look it,' added Jim, eyeing his friend's flaming red cheeks. 'You look exactly like an overblown peony, Freddy.'

'You don't look much better yourself,' retorted the journalist.

'In fact,' said Jim, 'the only person who

looks really cool is Miss Orde.'

'Well, she doesn't feel it,' said that lady, stopping and extracting a powder puff and mirror from her handbag. 'All my clothes are sticking to me and I'm sure my face must be a sight.'

'It is,' said Jim gallantly. 'A sight for the gods.'

'I ought to reply to that in the language of the 'gods',' said the girl, busily powdering her nose, 'but I was well brought up.'

'And anyway you can't do it,' put in Freddy. 'You know you've tried over and over again, and the result has been lamentable.'

They continued up the little path, and presently sighting a felled tree, Jim suggested a rest and a smoke. His suggestion was agreed to with alacrity.

'Whoever suggested this walk,' said Freddy Kemp a few moments later, seated astride the tree trunk, 'deserves some kind of medical attention.'

'You suggested it yourself,' said Phil, holding her cigarette in the flame of the match that Jim held out.

'If I did I must have been crazy,' said the journalist, 'but I'm sure I didn't. If I remember right it was you.'

'Your memory's failing you, darling,' said the girl, blowing out a cloud of smoke and watching it disperse slowly in the still air. 'I've noticed it before. I'm afraid you're gradually breaking up.'

'Another afternoon like this and I shall be broken up!' grunted Freddy. 'Phew! What wouldn't I give for a pint of beer straight off the ice!'

'It would only make you hotter,' said the girl practically.

'It couldn't,' declared Freddy fervently. 'Hell itself couldn't make me any hotter than I am at present.'

'Well, it's a good thing to get acclimatised,' said Jim. 'Personally I don't think it is so bad — '

He broke off as Phyllis uttered a little warning hiss, and following the direction of her eyes, saw approaching them up the winding path a dapper figure in grey flannels. The newcomer was a good way away from them, but even at that distance there was no mistaking who he was.

He was hatless, and the grey hair with the strands of white showed up with startling clearness against the deep tan of his face. It was Patterson-Willis. He came on slowly, his hands clasped behind his back, his eyes fixed on the ground. It was clear that he had not as yet seen them, and Jim watched him as he approached, glad of this unexpected opportunity to see more of the owner of Lady's Manor.

'Good afternoon, Dr. Patterson-Willis,' he said. 'What a lovely day!'

The doctor looked at him, his smoke-grey eyes half veiled by his large lids.

'Good afternoon,' he grunted. 'It's beautiful, isn't it?' and as he spoke Jim saw something that made him give a little inward start.

A suspicion that almost amounted to a certainty crossed his mind.

'I suppose to you,' he continued, 'having just come back from abroad, this weather is child's play.'

'Eh? Oh, yes, of course,' replied the doctor.

He was continuing on his way when Jim called sharply.

'Which day is cheese day?'

'Wednesday,' said the other instantly and unthinkingly, and then realising what he had said he stopped dead, shot Jim a venomous look, and then continued down the winding path at a slightly increased pace.

'What the dickens did you mean by that?' gasped Freddy Kemp, his round face the picture of astonishment. 'Which day is cheese day? Has the heat sent you crazy?'

'No, I'm quite sane, thank you,' replied Jim staring after the retreating figure in grey. 'I've just confirmed a suspicion that occurred to me concerning Patterson-Willis, that's all.'

16

Phyllis Orde investigates

The window of Phyllis Orde's bedroom in the little cottage was one of those small casement affairs that open outwards. Below it was a box-ottoman, covered with chintz to match the curtains, and with both halves of the window flung wide to the night the girl sat on this and stared out into the cool darkness. The threatened storm had not yet materialised. The sky was overcast by heavy banks of clouds, and a faint breeze stirred the leaves of the trees fitfully. If the storm had not yet broken it was not far off. That intangible something that heralds the approach of thunder was making the atmosphere thick and heavy.

Phil pushed the hair back from her forehead and let what breeze there was play on her face. She felt restless and wakeful. Perhaps it was the after effects of the intense heat of the day, perhaps the result of the electrically charged air: whatever the cause, she had never felt less like sleep in her life. It was barely half-past ten, but Mrs. Jillider and her husband had long since retired for the night. The girl had come up to her room with the intention of going to bed and reading herself to sleep, but as yet she had not even attempted to light her candle.

The darkness outside looked very alluring, and she let it bathe her eyes to rid them of the strain of the day's sun. For some time she sat on thinking, and her thoughts turned, naturally enough, to the reason for her being in the little cottage at all. She was intensely interested in the whole affair, and not for the first time since she had left Jim and Freddy she wondered what the young Inspector had meant by his cryptic words, 'Which day is cheese day?'

It seemed such a perfectly absurd thing to say, and yet Dr. Patterson-Willis had evidently not thought so, for he had answered at once and without hesitation, 'Wednesday'. Now, what on earth could it mean! Jim had said that it had confirmed a suspicion that he had entertained regarding the doctor, but although Phil racked her brains she couldn't think how.

As a natural sequence to this line of thought she began to think about Lady's Manor and its inhabitants. Freddy had told her about his and Jim's adventures on the previous night and of the shadowy figure they had seen on the blind. Was this really the home of the queer-faced man who came forth under cover of darkness and prowled about in the woods and lanes surrounding the little village? If so, perhaps he was even at that moment preparing to set forth on a nocturnal excursion.

She knew that Jim and Freddy had no intention of going to Lady's Manor that night, they were both tired, and had decided to put off further investigation of that mysterious house until after the inquest, but there was nothing to prevent her going. Her eyes sparkled with excitement as the idea entered her brain. The stuffy little bedroom suddenly became almost unbearable, and the darkness of the night beckoned her. The exercise at least would do her good, and probably bring on the sleepiness that now seemed so far away, and apart from this she might discover something. It would be rather wonderful if she could. She pictured the astonishment on the faces of Jim and Freddy if she confronted them on the following morning with vital information that would help them to clear up the mystery.

The idea, which at first had been but a fleeting one, gradually took hold of her, and quite suddenly she made up her mind, and decided to put it into execution. Rising to her feet she lit her candle and proceeded to set about making her preparations for the outing. Exchanging the high-heeled shoes she was wearing for a pair of brogues, she slipped over her light summer frock a dark-coloured mackintosh, a beret, into which she tucked the straying strands of her hair completing her attire. Picking up the candle she opened the door and tiptoed noiselessly out into the passage.

As silently as she could she crept down the narrow staircase and setting down the candle on a chair in the tiny hall, began cautiously to pull back the chain and the bolt on the front door. In a few seconds it was open, and blowing out the candle she passed through, closing the door softly behind her. Her heart was beating fast with excitement as she walked down the crazy pavement, opened the gate leading on to the road, and slipped through.

Walking quickly, she reached the beginning of the rise that led up to the gates of Dead Trees. The little breeze, which she had heard and felt from her window, had died away. A profound stillness seemed to have settled on the world, or rather this part of it in which she was immediately concerned.

She reached Dead Trees and looked at the forbidding entrance. There was no sight or sound of life, and passing it she turned into the lane, which led to Lady's Manor. She was a yard away from the iron gate that led to the drive when she stopped suddenly and crouched back into the shelter of the hedge, almost holding her breath. She had heard the click of the latch, and she knew by the sound that someone was opening the gate. Her eyes had grown more accustomed to the darkness by now, and straining them to their utmost she peered at the dim white blur which marked the stone pillars between which the gate hung, A dark shadow obscured one as someone stepped out into the lane, and the vision was followed almost instantly by a faint clang as the gate swung to behind the person who had come out. She could not see who it was, but she hoped that they would not look in her direction as they passed her. As it turned out, this fear was groundless, for the night walker moved slowly away in the opposite direction. She heard his footsteps stumbling over the rough surface of the lane, and with the blood in her veins tingling she began stealthily to follow the sound. Her eyes were aching with the effort to see into the blackness ahead, but now she could see nothing, and had to trust entirely to her sense of hearing.

The lane ended abruptly, and she suddenly found herself in the midst of tree trunks. They grew thickly, and she found it difficult to proceed, for there was no path. The footsteps ahead of her were slower now, and all at once a splash of light appeared in the darkness, and she saw that the person she was following had switched on a torch. The irregular pool of whiteness danced on the ground before him.

In the reflected light she was able to see his figure clearly. He was a tall man, and looked thin, but this may have been due to the distortion of the light. He was dressed in a lounge suit of some dark material and wore a soft hat. Under his left arm he carried a bulky package. With the torch as a guide, following him was easy. Without looking to right or to left, and apparently totally unaware that his footsteps were being dogged, he hurried through the wood at a pace that the girl found difficult to keep up with.

Presently the trees began to thin, and a few yards farther on they came out into open country. The ground began to rise steeply, and presently they struck a little path that ran along the edge of a wood that covered the towering hillside to the right. Phil had no idea where she was, and for the matter of that her exact location never crossed her mind. Her entire faculties were concentrated on the man in front. She was curious to know the destination of this midnight excursion, and it was not very long before her curiosity was to be satisfied.

They had traversed about two hundred yards of the winding path when the man she was following came to an abrupt stop. For a moment she thought he had heard her, and her heart leaped into her mouth. Near at hand was a ragged patch of thickly growing bushes, and dropping behind these so that they effectually screened her, she watched to see what he would do next. What he did do was a disappointment, for he put out the torch. She could see nothing now, and had to trust once more to her ears. Listening intently she heard faintly the sound of tearing paper and guessed that he was opening the parcel that he had been carrying under his arm. Her wonderment and curiosity increased. Why on earth did he come all this way, in order to open that parcel.

The sound of tearing paper ceased and was followed after a few seconds by the unmistakable ringing of metal against metal, and then across the blackness of the sky flickered a ribbon of blue. In the glare of the lightning she caught a momentary impression of the man she had been following bending over an object that resembled a squat tripod, and then darkness blotted out the vision. She waited, hoping that the lightning would come again, and presently it did.

There was a low muttering rumble of distant thunder, and then another and brighter flash than the one before. Fastened to the tripod now was a long, barrel-like thing that resembled a telescope. Once more came darkness, and she puzzled her brain to account for the curious-looking contrivance. If it was a telescope what was the man going to do with it? How could he hope to see anything on a night as dark as this?

A reverberating roll of thunder startled her. It was followed almost instantly by a vivid white radiance that for a fraction of a second illumined the whole countryside with a light as bright as the brightest noon. She saw the dark figure of the unknown man bending over his curious contraption and saw also something else. On the other side of the valley-like depression, and in almost a direct line with the barrel of the instrument he had erected on the hillside was the back of the Load of Hay.

17

Just in Time

Jim finished his whiskey and soda, set down the empty glass, and looked across at Freddy Kemp, who was engaged on his sixth unsuccessful game of patience.

'I'm for a spot of bed,' he remarked, rising to his feet.

'Same here,' grunted Freddy. 'I think it'll come out this time.'

'It ought to,' said Jim. 'I've been watching you, and you've deliberately cheated three times. A man who can cheat himself at patience is capable of anything.'

The big journalist grinned, swept the cards together, stacked, them neatly and replaced them in their box.

'I said I wouldn't go to bed until I got a game out,' he replied. 'And since I'm dead tired, and to keep my word it looked as if I should have to remain here for the best part of the night, I chose the lesser of two evils. Come on, let's make tracks for the virtuous couch.'

Jim blew out the lamp and followed his friend out to the passage. The rest of the inhabitants of the Load of Hay had been in bed for some time, for it was getting on for twenty to twelve. Outside Jim's door Freddy wished the young Inspector goodnight and moved further along the passage to his own room. Entering his bedroom Jim closed the door and fumbled in his pockets for a box of matches. He found it, struck one, and looked about him for the candle, which usually stood upon a little table beside the bed. Tonight, however, it had been moved for some reason and put over by the window on the dressing table. As he located it the match smouldered out. He was just in the act of striking another when a glare of lightning lit up the room and he paused. So the storm had broken at last, had it? Well, it was a good thing, thought Jim. It would clear the air and counteract the unhealthy heat of the last few days.

He dropped the matches back into his pocket. If there was one thing he enjoyed more than another it was to watch a thunderstorm. The most wonderful sight he ever had seen in his life had been a storm at sea. He perched himself on the sill of the open window and stared out.

The storm as yet was a good way off, but the time lapse between the first flash and its accompanying crash of thunder warned him that it was drawing nearer. For some time he watched contentedly the grandest sight that nature can provide, then, as the first patter of rain began to fall, he decided that he had had enough. He took out his matches again with the intention of lighting his candle, and had half-risen from the windowsill when he heard a voice calling urgently from below.

'Mr. Brent!' it said breathlessly. 'Mr. Brent!'

Wondering what on earth the girl was doing there, he leaned out of the window.

'What is it?' he called.

'Don't strike that match,' she said.

Obviously, in the momentary flash she

had seen the box in his hand, and filled with a great wonderment Jim leaned further out the window. 'Why not?'

'Never mind,' panted the girl. 'Don't. Come down, Mr. Brent, I must see you.'

'All right,' said the still bewildered Jim. 'Wait a minute while I light the candle — '

'No, don't light the candle,' cried Phyllis, hoarsely. 'Find your way in the dark, but come down, Mr. Brent.'

The girl's tone was so urgent that Jim refrained from further argument. Going to the door he opened it and made his way downstairs. A passage ran from the hall of the inn to a door, which opened into the garden. Pulling back the bolt he turned the latch and stepped out into the now rapidly falling rain. The girl joined him instantly.

'What's all this mystery about?' he demanded. 'Why is it so essential that I shouldn't show a light?'

She was still panting heavily and it was some seconds before she could answer him.

'There's a man up on the hillside,' she

spoke rapidly and jerkily, 'and he's got some kind of a gun trained on this place. I thought at first it was a telescope, and then in the lightning I saw him open the breech and put in a thing like a cartridge.'

Jim stared at her, his astonishment increasing.

'Up there?' he said, waving his hand in the direction of the rising hill.

She nodded.

'But what in the world were you doing up there to see him?' he asked.

As briefly as possible she related her adventure of the night, and Jim whistled softly.

'The moment I guessed what it was,' she concluded, 'I thought I'd better warn you, and I scrambled down the hillside and across the meadows. It took me less than ten minutes.'

'You've done wonders,' said Jim admiringly. 'Now, wait a minute and let me think.'

He drew her out of the rain into the shadow of the porch, and rapidly considered the situation. Somewhere out there in the darkness of the storm, unless

Phyllis Orde had been mistaken, was a man with a gun trained on to the back of the Load of Hay, waiting, presumably to put a bullet through Jim as he lit his candle. On consideration, Jim saw that it was rather an optimistic proceeding. To start with, he might have gone to bed early, before the man had arrived with the weapon, and for another, the distance was so considerable that even an expert shot would find it impossible to be certain of hitting his target. The whole thing, looked at in the light of reason, seemed absurd.

'You're sure you weren't mistaken about this gun, Miss Orde?' he asked, and the girl shook her head vigorously.

'No,' she answered. 'He switched on the torch to make sure that he had got everything fixed up, and if I hadn't been certain before I should have been then. It's a gun right enough, but it's not like an ordinary gun. The barrel's bigger and thicker.'

'Well,' said Jim after a moment's silence. 'We've got to risk it.'

'What do you mean?' she asked.

'I mean that I'm going to find out

exactly what this fellow's idea is,' he replied. 'Now, you go round to the front of the inn and wait till I join you.'

She would have liked to question him as to what he was going to do, but there was something in the tone of Jim's voice at that moment that prohibited all argument, and with a nod she turned to obey his instructions. When she had gone he re-entered the inn, ascended the stairs, and pushed open the door of his room. Her description of the gun had suggested a vague theory to him and he intended to put it to the test.

Entering the room in the dark he felt his way over to the dressing table and picked up the candle. Carrying it back into the passage, he closed the door, and striking a match lit it. After a second's hesitation he re-entered the room again, walked swiftly over to the window, put the lighted candle down on the dressing table, and running out of the room, closed the door quickly behind him and hurried down the stairs. Reaching the garden he stood in the drenching rain waiting and listening for confirmation of his theory, and he didn't have long to wait. A crash of thunder shook the earth, almost simultaneously with a dazzling flash of lightning, and as the echoing rumble of it died to silence there came a muffled explosion from the room above. An echo, or what sounded like an echo, sharp and staccato, came from the distant hillside.

Jim raced back up the stairs, and holding his handkerchief to his mouth pushed open his door an inch. A peculiar smell reached his nostrils, and he pulled it shut with a bang. A second later he was hammering the door of Freddy Kemp's room.

A sleepy voice demanded to know what was the matter.

'Open the door!' snapped Jim, 'and look sharp about it!'

He heard the creak of a bed, followed by the padding of naked feet and then the key turned and the door was jerked open. Freddy Kemp's red face, his hair tousled, glared out at him.

'What the dickens is the matter?' he demanded grumpily. 'Is there a fire?'

'No. Something almost worse,' said Jim

grimly. 'My room's full of poison gas.'

The journalist's jaw dropped and his sleep-laden eyes stared in astonishment.

'Poison gas?' he repeated stupidly. 'How did it get there? How — ?'

'Never mind the questions,' snapped Jim. 'Put your things on as quickly as you can and come downstairs, and hold your breath as you pass my door. Luckily, no one else sleeps on this floor.'

'I don't suppose it will take long to disperse,' gasped Jin as after hurriedly undoing the front door he released his pent-up breath. 'But we'd better wake the landlady and Joyce and get them out of the place until the stuff's blown away. The barmaid sleeps over the garage, so she's all right.'

'What's happened?' asked the voice of Phyllis Orde excitedly, and she appeared out of the darkness.

'Phil!' gasped Freddy. 'What on earth are you doing here?'

'Don't wait to ask questions, man!' said Jim impatiently. 'Go and wake Mrs. Lanning and the girl.'

The journalist hurried away and Jim

answered the girl's flood of questions.

'Poison gas!' she repeated in a horrified voice. 'But — I don't — understand.'

'The gun you saw contained a small shell of compressed gas,' explained Jim. 'A very virulent gas I should say, since it was intended to take effect instantly before I had time to realise what had happened and run from the room.'

'How horrible!' said the girl, and her voice quivered.

'Horrible!' agreed Jim, 'but extremely ingenious. I've no doubt the man who fired that gun thought I was already in bed and asleep. He couldn't have been waiting for a light to let off his infernal machine.'

Before she could say any more Freddy Kemp returned, marshalling the frightened figures of the landlady and the rosy-cheeked housemaid.

Jim stopped Mrs. Lanning's excited flow of questions and thrust both of the women into the bar parlour.

'You go and pacify them,' he said to Phil, and taking Kemp's arm led him into the bar.

'Have you got a handkerchief?' he asked, and the journalist produced one from his breast pocket.

Jim took it, and together with his own soaked it thoroughly in one of the jugs of water standing on the counter.

'Tie this round your nose and mouth,' he said, handing the dripping handkerchief back to Freddy, and proceeded to do the same with his own.

Equipped in their improvised gas masks, they went back up the stairs, and Jim threw the door of his room wide, and opened the two windows on the landing. Even with the protection of the soaked handkerchief he suddenly felt a wave of dizziness attack him, and grabbing Freddy by the arm hurried the journalist down the stairs.

'That's the best we can do for the moment,' he said, speaking with difficulty through the folds of the wet cambric, 'and I think it would be safer if we got everybody out of the place until the last remnant of the stuff, whatever it is, has dispersed.'

He went to the door of the little

parlour, and calling to Phil made her take the alarmed and expostulating Mrs. Lanning and the frightened girl to Mrs. Jellider's cottage. The landlady flatly refused to leave the inn at first, but when Jim told her that the place was full of poison gas she made no further demur, and indeed was in such a hurry to go that she was at the gate before Phil could catch up with her.

'What are we going to do?' demanded the journalist when they had gone. 'Spend the night in the rain?'

'No,' said Jim. 'There's a tool-shed at the bottom of the garden; it's small but dry.'

He led the way, and presently, seated on an old crate with Freddy reclining at his ease in a wheelbarrow, he related to the curious journalist exactly what had happened.

'What a diabolical idea!' exclaimed Kemp. 'Bit of luck for you that Phil was on the warpath.'

'It was,' admitted Jim. 'But for her, I think the scheme would have come off.'

'Well, they've tried twice,' grunted

Freddy. 'They certainly seem pretty anxious to get rid of you.'

'I think my remark to Patterson-Willis was mostly the cause of tonight's little episode,' answered Jim.

'D'you know,' said Freddy Kemp, 'I've been puzzling my brain ever since to know what you meant. What exactly is the significance of 'Which day is cheese day'? and why should Willis have answered 'Wednesday'?'

'It's really quite simple,' replied Jim with a grin. 'I'd have told you before only it rather tickled me to see your mystification. Did you notice any peculiarity about Patterson-Willis when you saw him this afternoon?'

'No,' said the journalist. 'What peculiarity did you notice?'

'I noticed when he was speaking,' answered the young Inspector, 'that he spoke out of one corner of his mouth. It was that that prompted my remark about the cheese.'

He paused and the journalist grunted.

'Go on, I'll buy it,' he growled.

'The prisons in this country,' explained

Jim, 'have a limited diet, and on certain days of the week supper consists of bread and cheese. It's considered quite a delicacy by the convicts, and each prison has a different day, which is rigidly adhered to. For instance, Maidstone's day is Friday, Chelmsford's Tuesday, and so on.'

'Do you mean,' exclaimed Freddy Kemp, 'that Dr. Patterson-Willis is an ex-convict!'

Jim nodded.

'I'm sure he is,' he replied. 'It's the convict's trick to speak out of the corner of his mouth, he does so to ensure that the prison guards can't catch him. Yes, Patterson-Willis may be an authority on skin diseases, and he may have spent a lot of his time abroad, but at one time in his life he was in Princetown Prison. Cheese day in Dartmoor is on Wednesday.'

18

A Report from the Yard

The storm was past and the sun was well up before Jim, after a third voyage of exploration from the tool shed to the inn, reported that the last vestige of gas had dispersed. Sending Freddy Kemp round to Phyllis Orde's cottage to give the landlady the 'All clear', he went up to his bedroom and made an examination. A faint chemical smell still clung about the curtains and the bedding, but the air was quite fresh and breathable.

'Everything's all right now, Mrs. Lanning,' he said cheerily. 'And practically no damage has been done.'

'What really happened, Mr. Brent?' asked the landlady, curiously. 'Was someone playing a trick on yer?'

'Yes, I think they were,' said Jim, a little grimly.

'Well it was a stupid thing to do,' said

Mrs. Lanning, shaking her head. 'It might have been serious.'

Jim thought it might have been very serious indeed, but he had no wish to enlarge upon the incident, so he passed the matter off.

'I expect you'd like your breakfast as soon as possible, sir,' said Mrs. Lanning. 'I'll just have a bit of a wash, to wake myself up like, and then see about it.' She called to the yawning Joyce, who had accompanied her, and bustled away.

'I think I'll follow our good landlady's suggestion,' remarked Freddy Kemp. 'It's a long time since I spent a night in a toolshed and I think a wash is indicated.'

He went upstairs to his room, and Jim, left alone, strolled out into the garden.

The morning was lovely. The storm had wiped away the humid and almost tropical heat of the past few days, and although it was fine and warm there was a freshness in the air which was very pleasant. Jim drew great gulps of it into his lungs, and pondered on the incident of the night. He was still pondering when

Freddy, his face smooth and shining, joined him.

'There's a most delectable smell coming from the kitchen department,' he declared rubbing his hands, 'and what I could do to a plate of kidneys and bacon is nobody's business.'

'I could toy daintily with a piece of toast myself,' replied Jim.

At that moment Joyce called them and they made their way with alacrity to the coffee room. Over the appetising meal they discussed the fresh development.

'I should think you have got enough evidence to arrest Patterson-Willis,' said Freddy, speaking with difficulty, his mouth full of kidney and bacon. 'You're pretty certain he's an ex-convict, and Phil's evidence proves that this fellow who tried to do the dirty on you came from Lady's Manor.'

'I think there's ample evidence to detain Willis on suspicion,' answered Jim, 'but I'm not so sure it would be a good move. It's the other man I'm after, Freddy, this fellow with the queer face, and if we go after Patterson-Willis he might quite easily give us the slip.'

'What do you propose doing then?' asked the journalist, helping himself to another piece of toast.

'At the moment,' said Jim, 'I think we'll adopt the policy of masterly inactivity. I don't think Miss Orde was spotted last night, and if she wasn't this fellow won't know that we have the least suspicion he came from Lady's Manor. He'll just think that his little plan went astray.'

'You don't think there's any danger of them clearing out?' asked Kemp, and Jim shook his head.

'I don't think there's the slightest danger,' he answered, 'while Hillbury remains at Dead Trees. He's the game they're after, for some reason or other, and unless we do something to thoroughly scare them, they're going to play it out. These attacks on me are a sideline, but the main object is Hillbury.'

'I wonder why they're after him,' muttered Kemp, frowning. 'What can he have done?'

'I'd like to know that,' said Jim. 'It must be something pretty bad, for he's frightened to death of this queer faced man, that's why he's gone to ground in that unpleasant house of his.'

Joyce entered as he finished speaking, and handed him a bulky envelope.

'The postman's just brought it, sir,' she announced unnecessarily.

'I expect this is from the Yard,' said Jim, when the girl had gone, and ripped open the flap.

Enclosed was a letter from Chief Inspector Mason with several typewritten sheets. A hasty glance showed Jim that these were reports, and laying them aside, he read the letter.

New Scotland Yard,
London, S. W. I.
21st June, 1934.

90/A. L. P./724/P.M.
Dear Brent,

I've done what I can to answer the questions contained in your letter.

With regard to Lesley Allerton, see enclosed report L.P./1042960

The thumbprint on the knife handle

corresponds exactly with the one found on the gear lever of the launch belonging to the unknown murderer at Bourne End.

I can find no trace or record of Hillbury, but your description might apply to a man known as Lewis Gleeson. This man is suspected of being a fence and a trafficker in dangerous drugs. Eighteen months ago he disappeared from his usual haunts, and there has been no trace of him since.

I enclose (see R.O./5923S60) everything that is known about this man on the chance that he might be your Mr. Hillbury.

I think you've struck a mare's-nest in Dr. Patterson-Willis. This man has a very high reputation, and nothing at all is known against him. He is one of the leading specialists in skin diseases, and for some time had a large practice in Harley Street. He retired from this six years ago in order to devote his time to research work, and he is a man of considerable wealth.

Let me know what progress you're making, and if you require any help.

Yours sincerely,

R. MASON, Chief Inspector.

Jim put down the letter and picked up the typewritten sheets. Each report was clipped together, separately, and he turned his attention first to the one concerning Lesley Allerton. It contained very little information, but what there was, was helpful.

A girl named Lesley Allerton, who had been living in a boarding house at Bayswater, had, eight months ago, mysteriously disappeared. She had gone out one evening to post a letter and had not returned. The landlady of the boarding house had notified the police the following day, and although every effort had been made to trace her, they had been unable to do so. No photograph was available, but a description of the girl as supplied by the landlady at the time was appended.

The report on Lewis Gleeson was more interesting. His description exactly fitted

Mr. Hillbury, and as Jim read all that was known about the man he became more and more convinced that Hillbury and Gleeson were one and the same, and this conviction became a certainty when, towards the end of the report, he discovered that Gleeson had married a woman known as Myra Delmonte who had been a hostess at a West End dancing club.

'That's our Mr. Hillbury,' he said to Freddy Kemp. 'Lewis Gleeson. Suspected by the Yard of being a fence and a trafficker in dangerous drugs. To that I think I may add, a kidnapper of young girls.'

'We seem to be getting on,' said the journalist.

'We are,' replied Jim, 'but we've got a long way to go yet. We are no nearer to discovering the identity of the queer-faced man, or why Hillbury, or Gleeson, is afraid of him.'

'Well, Patterson-Willis seems to be out of it anyway,' remarked Freddy. 'You made a bloomer about his having been in prison, Jim. If he had they'd have had a record of it at headquarters.'

'I suppose I was mistaken,' said Jim, but his voice lacked conviction. 'And yet, why did he answer 'Wednesday' when I asked him that question about the cheese?'

The journalist shrugged his broad shoulders.

'It seems queer,' he agreed. 'The only thing I can suggest is that he knew something about prison systems and just answered the question.'

'But as I've told you,' said Jim, 'every prison has a different day. Why should he have chosen Dartmoor? No; I don't think that explains it; there's a simpler explanation, to my mind.'

'What's that?' asked Freddy.

'That the man isn't Patterson-Willis at all,' answered Jim, looking at his friend steadily. 'That the real Patterson-Willis is still abroad, and that this man, for reasons of his own, has taken his place.'

19

Strangers in the Village

It was a startling suggestion, but the more they discussed it, the more feasible it became. If Patterson-Willis was a man of such high standing — and there seemed little doubt of this, for Scotland Yard as a rule did not make mistakes — it was inconceivable that he should have become mixed up with the queer faced man and the whole extraordinary business surrounding Hillbury, Dead Trees, and the murder of Dan Killick. There was, of course, always the possibility that he was being forced into something against his will. There might have been something in his past, unknown to the world, which had come into the possession of the jewel robber and murderer, which he was using to blackmail the doctor into doing his business. At the same time, this did not account for the old lag's trick of speaking out of the corner of his mouth, and for his instantaneous answer to Jim's question. This could only be accounted for by the fact that the Patterson-Willis they knew and the real Patterson-Willis were two separate and distinct personalities. There was one snag against this, however, which Freddy Kemp pointed out.

Why, if Patterson-Willis was not Patterson-Willis, had he agreed so readily, when the *Clarion* had rung him up, to grant an interview!

'He didn't grant it, did he?' said Jim. 'And the reason he changed his mind so quickly is explainable if he was an imposter. He couldn't possibly give you an interview because he was ignorant of his subject.'

'Then why not have said so straight away when the paper rung him up?' argued Kemp. 'It was quite easy for him to make an excuse. He could have said that he was busy, that he didn't want to be disturbed — dozens of things. Why jump at the suggestion more or less eagerly?'

'I'm afraid I can't tell you,' said Jim,

rising to his feet, 'but I expect he had a very good reason. Now we'd better get along to the inquest.'

The inquiry was being held in the schoolroom, and practically the entire population of Little Siltley had turned up to enjoy the unexpected and unusual excitement. The place was packed, and as Jim, accompanied by Freddy Kemp and Phyllis Orde, reached the building, a big closed car drew into the kerb and deposited the stout and perspiring figure of Mr. Hillbury.

'I bet it costs him an effort to leave his stronghold,' chuckled Freddy Kemp, as they followed in the wake of the fat man. 'So that's Hillbury, is it? A most unpleasant specimen. I should think he was capable of anything.'

The proceedings, as Jim had expected, were very brief. The medical evidence and the identity of the victim were taken briefly and then, to the disappointment of the gaping sightseers, the proceedings were adjourned for a fortnight. Jim waited behind to talk to Laker, and presently succeeded in getting that rather harassed official to himself.

'I've got some news from the Yard that may interest you,' he said, and proceeded to acquaint the Superintendent with the gist of the report he had received that morning.

Laker was interested.

'I'd like to go into this more fully, Mr. Brent,' he said, 'but we can't talk here. Can you come down to the station?'

Jim nodded.

'I've just got to have a word with the Coroner,' said the Superintendent, 'and then I'll come back.'

Jim waited, talking to Freddy Kemp and Phyllis Orde.

'Did you see Hillbury go?' asked the journalist. 'He bolted for his life immediately the proceedings ended.'

'Anxious to get back to his fortress, I suppose,' said Jim. 'That fellow oozes terror at every pore.'

The girl, who had been rather silent and thoughtful that morning, turned to Jim suddenly.

'Mr. Brent,' she said, 'I've got an idea, and if you will let me do it, I think it might lead to something.'

'Spill it, Miss Orde,' said Jim briefly.

'Well,' said the girl eagerly, 'you know those two servants at Hillbury's house?'

'Yes,' said Jim.

'They've never seen me,' said the girl rapidly, 'and I've been talking to Mrs. Jillider and she says that they take a walk, one in the morning and one in the afternoon. Not together but separately. Supposing I happen to be in the vicinity and get into conversation with one of them — '

'Get off with him, d'you mean?' grunted Freddy bluntly.

She nodded.

'Yes, if you like to put it so vulgarly,' she answered. 'Don't you think I might learn something?'

Jim frowned and scratched his chin.

'I think it's very doubtful, Miss Orde,' he said presently, after a pause,

'But still I might,' persisted the girl. 'There's no harm in trying.'

'I think it's a rotten idea,' said Freddy Kemp decisively. 'Going around flirting with ex-bruisers — '

'It's only a matter of business,' she said smiling. 'You needn't be jealous.'

The colour in the journalist's large red face deepened.

'I'm not jealous,' he growled, 'but I don't think you ought to do it. It might lead to a lot of unpleasantness.'

The girl's chin set obstinately.

'I'm quite capable of taking care of myself,' she said, 'so you needn't worry about that part. What do you think? Mr. Brent?'

'I'm rather in agreement with Freddy,' he replied. 'I don't think I like the idea.'

'But you must admit that it might lead to something,' she insisted.

'Yes, I admit that,' said Jim reluctantly. 'But — '

'Then I'm going to try it,' she said. 'What's the good of my being here if I don't make myself useful?'

Jim looked at Freddy, and the journalist shrugged his shoulders. They both knew from experience that when Phyllis Orde made up her mind it was useless arguing, and, as Jim had said, it might lead to something. A man might talk freely to an attractive girl, particularly if he had no suspicion of her, and neither of the two guardians of Mr. Hillbury's safety were likely to be suspicious of such an innocent looking person as Phyllis Orde.

Before they could say any more, Laker came back.

'Are you ready?' he said, and at Jim's nod led the way out to the street. Here they parted from Freddy Kemp and the girl and walked in the opposite direction towards the little station house.

Seated in the Superintendent's office, Jim produced the reports that he had received that morning, and Laker read them with interest.

'There seems very little doubt,' said the Superintendent, 'that this fellow Hillbury is the Gleeson mentioned here. If I remember rightly, he called that wife of his Myra.'

'You remember quite rightly,' said Jim. 'He did, and apart from that, the description fits him exactly. I've very little doubt myself that Hillbury and Gleeson are one and the same man.'

'It's worth knowing, but it doesn't give

us a lot of help,' grunted Laker. 'The Yard people apparently have got nothing against Gleeson except suspicion, so we can't very well interfere with him. You see I was right about Patterson-Willis.'

'I think you were right about the real Patterson-Willis,' said Jim slowly, 'but I don't think the real Patterson-Willis is at Lady's Manor.'

'What! Do you mean that the man there is an imposter?' he gasped incoherently.

'I'm pretty sure of it,' said Jim. 'Listen.'

He hitched his chair nearer to the desk, and resting his arms on the flat top began rapidly to tell the Superintendent of the man he had seen in the wood on the night of Dan Killick's murder, his own adventures in the grounds of Dead Trees, his visit with Freddy Kemp to Lady's Manor, and the shadow of the man they had seen on the blind, concluding with an account of the gas shell which had been fired from the hillside into his room at the inn.

'I wish you'd told me this before, Mr. Brent,' he said frowning. 'I don't think you ought to have kept it back. I could have taken some action — '

'That's just why I kept it back,' interrupted Jim. 'It was because I was afraid that you would insist on taking action that I didn't tell you before.'

Laker was ruffled, and it took some time before Jim succeeded in smoothing him down.

'So you think,' said the Superintendent presently, 'that this man who has taken the place of Patterson-Willis is an old lag?'

'I do,' replied Jim. 'My theory is this. Patterson-Willis is still abroad, and these people commandeered Lady's Manor in order to be near Dead Trees.'

'I'm inclined to agree with you,' said Laker, 'and I think the best thing we can do is go up there and arrest him right away.'

'I wouldn't do that if I were you,' said Jim hastily. 'You might get the man who is masquerading as Patterson-Willis and the black man, but I think you'd lose the fellow we're after. He's clever, this queer faced man, don't forget that. He was clever enough to commit a series of burglaries and get clean away with the proceeds.'

The Superintendent was unconvinced.

'You may be right,' he said thoughtfully, 'but, anyway, it's for the Chief Constable to decide. I shall have to lay the whole thing before him, of course.'

Jim compressed his lips. He did not want Colonel Lucas butting in. Excellent as that individual may have been in commands of a brigade in Poona, he could not imagine him doing anything else but making a mess of this affair. As tactfully as possible he suggested this to Laker, and the Superintendent was inclined to agree, but at the same time reminded Jim that the Colonel was his superior officer and that he was likely to get into serious trouble if Jim's discoveries were not reported.

It took Jim a solid hour of argument before he could shift Laker's opinion, and even then he only succeeded in effecting a compromise.

'I'll tell you what I'll do, Mr. Brent,' said the Superintendent. 'I won't say anything for three days, and during that time we'll work along your lines, but you mustn't keep anything more back.'

Jim agreed to this, he had no other option, and discovering that it was nearly lunchtime and that he was feeling hungry, took his leave of Laker and set off to walk back to the inn. Outside the tobacconist's in the High Street a big saloon car was drawn up, an opulent machine of shining cellulose and glittering chromium plate. It was an unusual sight in Little Siltley, and Jim stopped to admire. As he did so a little man in a chauffeur's uniform came hurrying out of the shop and almost cannoned into him.

'Sorry, guv'nor,' he said hastily, and then as he caught sight of Jim's face his jaw dropped, and muttering something below his breath he almost ran to the car. Before he could climb into the driving seat, however, Jim's hand had grasped him by the shoulder and dragged him back.

'Not so fast,' he said pleasantly. 'There's no need to be in such a hurry, Arty.'

The little man tried to wriggle free.

'You made a mistake, ain't yer?' he said; then: 'My name ain't Arty.'

'What are you calling yourself now, then?' asked Jim, still gripping him by the skinny shoulder. 'The last time I met you, you were Arty Smith, and you only escaped getting five years for burglary because your friends perjured themselves to provide you with an alibi.'

'All right, then,' said the other sullenly. 'I ain't arguing, you can let go my shoulder.'

Jim loosened his grasp, and the little wizened man rubbed the place tenderly.

'Got a grip on yer, ain't yer?' he said resentfully. 'Blimey, you busies are everywhere!'

'You get about a bit yourself, don't you, Arty?' remarked Jim. 'How did you come by this bandwagon, and what are you doing in Little Siltley?'

20

The Letter

'I'm going straight,' said the little man virtuously, ''h'onesty pays best in the long run.'

'How the devil did you know that there was an aitch in honesty?' asked Jim.

'I pronounced it,' said Arty Smith seriously.

'So you're going straight, are you?' Jim went on. 'I'll bet you are. As straight as a corkscrew.'

Mr. Smith's cunning face assumed an innocent expression.

'I'm telling you the truth,' he said earnestly. 'If I may never move from this spot, Mr. Brent. I've got a job now, shuvver to a rich gentleman.'

'How did you get it?' said Jim sceptically. 'Faked references?'

Arty Smith shook his head.

'No, 'e knows all about me,' he replied.

'I told 'im I was tired of being dishonest, and 'e offered to give me a fresh chance.'

'Sounds like something out of 'Aunt Agatha's Weekly',' said the disbelieving Jim. 'What's the name of this philanthropist?'

'Captain Freeman.' said Mr. Smith. 'E's a good feller. Got bags of dough. Look at that car,' he jerked his head towards the huge saloon. 'Cost fifteen 'undred, that did. I know, 'cause I went with 'im to buy it.'

'It is to be hoped,' said Jim, 'that he keeps his money under lock and key while you're around, otherwise he'll wake up one morning and find he's not so rich.'

'I wouldn't take a penny of 'is money,' declared Mr. Smith. ''E's done me a good turn, 'e 'as, and I wouldn't be so ungrateful as to bite the 'and what fed me.'

Jim looked at him and his eyes twinkled.

'You've been reading mushy books.' he accused, and then before the other could utter the protest that hovered on his tongue he went on: 'Where is this wonderful employer of yours?'

' 'E's gone to visit a pal of 'is,' answered Arty Smith. 'I dropped 'im at the 'ouse and then I'd run out of fags, so I popped along to get some. I'm going back to pick 'im up now.'

'Calling on a friend is he?' said Jim. 'Does this friend live in Little Siltley?'

Mr. Smith nodded.

'Yes, 'e does,' he said. 'What's the idea of all these questions?'

'Just friendly interest and curiosity,' answered Jim. 'When I meet an expert burglar like you, Arty, and find him running around in a posh uniform playing at being a chauffeur, I'm naturally curious.'

'Burgling's a thing of the past,' said Mr. Smith. 'I've gived all that up, I'm earning an h'onest living now and can look me feller men in the eye without a flinch.'

'I must say you do it very well,' murmured Jim with a shake of the head, 'but it doesn't go down with me. You're up to some trick or other. I should be careful if I were you, Arty. You only escaped last time by the skin of your teeth.'

'I escaped because I was innocent,' declared Mr. Smith. 'I was playing cards with some friends at the 'Wheatsheaf' at the time the burglary was committed, you know that, and they came forward and told the 'Beak'.'

'You were playing cards with Tony Foster, Mike Dilling and Luke Heal, and they perjured themselves to get you off.'

'That's libellous,' said Arty Smith, 'they could have you for that, Brent.'

'It might be slanderous, but it certainly isn't libellous,' pointed out Jim. 'But anyway, I'm only warning you, Smith. Watch your step!'

'The trouble with you busies,' said Arty Smith, 'is that you are so disbelieving. Can't a feller turn over a new leaf because I've gone wrong once or twice there ain't no reason why I should continue goin' wrong, is there?'

'There is a very good reason,' retorted Jim. 'A crook you were born, Arty Smith, and a crook you'll die, and you can't kid me with this reform stuff. I've met too many of your sort, and there isn't one of them who hasn't tried to stuff me up with the old story about going straight. You'd rather make five pounds dishonestly than earn a hundred by working for it, and you know that as well as I do.'

The little man's eyes snapped angrily.

'Well, I ain't goin' to argue with you, Brent,' he said. 'I've told you the truth, and if you don't believe me, well that's your business. You've got nothing on me anyhow.'

'Not at the moment,' added Jim, as the other turned away and climbed up behind the wheel of his resplendent car.

Jim stood watching it until it was out of sight, and then continued on his way. The chance meeting had given him cause for wonderment. What was the little burglar doing in the vicinity of Little Siltley? And who was the rich Captain Freeman who employed him? All this talk about going straight had not interested Jim at all, it was a gag worn threadbare by every crook in the country. Arty Smith was up to something, and Jim wondered whether it had any connection with the business of which he was engaged. It was possible that the little burglar's presence was merely a coincidence, but Jim was inclined to discountenance this. Who had the unknown Captain Freeman been visiting? The answer occurred to him almost before the question had formed itself in his mind. Freeman had been to see Mr. Hillbury at Dead Trees. He had no proof of this, but he was as certain as if Arty Smith had told him in so many words.

He had reached the inn and was just turning into the entrance when the big car passed him, travelling at a high speed. He caught a glimpse of the mysterious Freeman sitting in the back, a stoutish man with a heavy-jowled face. The vision was gone in a flash, but not before he had seen that the man's face was contorted with rage. Something had apparently upset Arty Smith's employer.

All thought of the little burglar and Captain Freeman was, however, wiped from his mind when he read the letter which he found waiting for him. It had come by the midday post, and the envelope was addressed in printed characters. Inside was a half-sheet of cheap notepaper, and on this had been scrawled:

'Go back to London and mind your own business. Your father died through poking his nose into my affairs. You will share the same fate unless you heed this warning.'

There was no signature, but Jim knew from whom the message had come. The unknown jewel thief and murderer, Queer Face.

21

Phyllis Orde tries the Glad Eye

Phyllis Orde came out of the little gate of Mrs. Jillider's cottage and turned in the direction of the rise that led up to Dead Trees. In spite of Jim's unfavourable reception of her scheme and Freddy Kemp's arguments and protests, she had made up her mind to carry it out.

The afternoon was a fine one. A pleasant breeze tempered the heat of the sun, and the atmosphere was no longer heavy and sultry as it had been on the previous day. She walked slowly until she came in sight of the entrance to Mr. Hillbury's house and then, seating herself on the grass-covered bank that edged the road, she lit a cigarette and waited.

A burly man stepped through, clad in an open-necked cricket shirt and flannel trousers. For a moment or two he stood talking to someone on the other side of the wicket, then it closed with a click, She heard a bolt re-shot, and the man who had come out began to walk slowly towards her. He was a distinctly unpleasant specimen of humanity. He had his hands in his pockets, and from his thick lips protruded the stub of a cigarette. She had once been to a rather low-down boxing booth with Freddy Kemp, and this man reminded her of some of the prizefighters. He was hatless, and his hair grew low on a receding forehead. His eyes, small and red-rimmed, were almost invisible beneath his coarse brows, and his nose was broad and flattened. He stared hard at her as he passed, and summoning all her courage Phil smiled.

He stopped immediately and faced her, but there was no answering smile on his ugly face.

'What are you doing here?' he demanded ungraciously.

Phil's heart was beating furiously, but she assumed what she hoped was a coy expression.

'I came out for a walk,' she said, 'but it's so hot that I thought I'd sit down and rest for a moment.'

He grunted and spat the cigarette-end into the roadway.

'I shouldn't rest there if I were you,' he growled. 'We don't like people hanging about the entrance of our house.'

Not a very good beginning, thought the girl, but she was determined not to give up without a further effort.

'Is that your house?' she asked, nodding towards the gates of Dead Trees.

'Not exactly my house, but I live there,' he replied. 'Why ask? You saw me come out, didn't yer?'

His small eyes were watching her suspiciously, but there was no friendliness in their depths.

'I didn't know you lived there,' she said smiling sweetly. 'You might have been paying a visit.'

Without answering the man called Sam took a cheap packet of cigarettes from his trousers pocket, stuck one between his thick lips, and lighted it. As he flicked away the used match Phil racked her brains desperately for something to say, anything that might prolong the interview and bring about that state of friendliness which she desired.

'It's very pretty round here, isn't it?' she said. 'Some of the most beautiful country I've ever seen.'

'You'll find it prettier further along the road,' he said, allowing a jerky stream of smoke to trickle through his broad nostrils.

'Oh, shall I?' said Phil. 'I suppose you know all the prettiest places round here.' She accompanied the remark with an inviting glance, but it fell upon stony ground.

'I've got no time to waste looking at places,' growled the stolid Sam, 'so I don't know any. But if you take my advice you'll clear off from here.'

Without another word he turned and continued on his way towards the village.

Phil looked after him and could have cried with mortification. Her plan, which had seemed so easy of accomplishment had failed. This man at any rate was having no truck with her. With a heightened colour she rose to her feet and hesitated. She had no desire to go back to Mrs. Jillider's and spend the rest of the glorious afternoon in the confines of her stuffy bedroom; less desire at the moment to seek out Freddy and Jim and be forced to report her failure. She decided to walk on past the gates of Dead Trees and out into the open country. She began to walk slowly along the road, and presently found herself at the entrance to the shady lane that led to Lady's Manor.

In spite of the breeze the sun was very hot, and her annoyance at the failure of her plan had not been conducive to coolness.

The lane looked shady and inviting, and she turned into it. It was very pleasant here. The dim, greenish light that percolated through the interlaced leaves above her head was a relief after the strong glare of the road. She strolled gently along and presently came to the iron gates that led up to the house. She knew that it was open, and at the sight an inspiration was born in her mind. Perhaps she might be able to learn something here that would retrieve her earlier failure and at least give her something to tell Jim and

Freddy when she got back. If she could find out anything further concerning the inhabitants of Lady's Manor it would mitigate to a large extent the amusement that she knew awaited her when she related her failure to vamp the pugilistic guardian of Mr. Hillbury's safety.

For a fraction of a second she hesitated and then slipped through the half open gate and began to make her way cautiously up the dark tunnel of the drive. Everything around was very still, and, as on that previous occasion when she had come here with Jim and Freddy, she experienced again that eerie sensation of lifelessness. Whereas on the road there had been the constant twitterings of birds in the trees, here everything was silent. A peculiar, unnatural silence that was like the lull before the first thunderclap.

She experienced a cold, sinking sensation in the pit of her stomach and stopped, half inclined to turn back, but the thought of facing the two men with nothing to report spurred her on. She crept up the remaining portion of the drive, keeping to the grass edging, fearful lest the slightest sound of her footsteps in that deadly stillness would give her presence away. She had no idea of what she was going to look for, she was just trusting to luck that she might find something that would turn out to be useful information. She reached the space where the drive spread out into the circular space occupied by the cypress tree and paused.

The house lay in the shade of its branches like a sleeping animal. There was no sight or sound of life.

A semi-circular border of shrubbery reached from the point where she stood at the back of the place, and forcing her way among the thickly growing bushes she followed it. It brought her out on to the narrow gravel path that circled the house, the same spot from which Freddy and Jim had seen the shadow on the blind. She remembered this and glanced up at the window. The blind was up and the window stared back at her, a black square of emptiness.

Suddenly she became conscious of a sound that broke the intense stillness. The low murmur of whispering voices. They seemed to come from somewhere quite close, and she eventually decided that the sound emanated from a point round the angle of the wall, and tiptoeing towards this and peering round the corner she discovered close at hand a window. It was apparently partly open, for now the voices were much louder. There were two of them, men's voices, and they were discussing something in a low tone. She would have liked to have been able to see into that room, but this was impossible, for against the light she would have been discovered immediately.

The next best thing was to hear what was being said, and crouching against the wall at the side of the window she strained her ears and listened.

The man who was speaking was Patterson-Willis; she recognised his voice, but she could only catch a word here and there.

'Finish and clear out . . . No good . . . That infernal policeman . . . Running the risk.'

Another voice broke in on the first, a

strange voice. It spoke in a peculiar husky intonation.

'Tomorrow night . . . Take Gleeson by surprise. We can . . . '

A shadow fell across the wall beside her. She heard a muttered exclamation, and swinging round saw the huge black man staring at her. With a gasp of fear she started to run, but his enormous hand reached out and gripped her by the shoulder.

'What are you doing here?' he grunted, and then, as she opened her mouth to scream he jerked her towards him and stifled the cry in her throat with his other hand,

'No, you don't!' he growled as she struggled violently to free herself.

'What is it? What is the matter, Nap?' cried a startled voice, and she saw Patterson-Willis looking out of the window.

'I found this gal spying, boss,' answered the black man. 'What shall I do with her?'

'Bring her inside,' ordered Patterson-Willis, and as the other obeyed and picked her up in his huge arms Phyllis

Orde caught sight of another figure behind the doctor's, a tall, thin man with a white face, featureless and horrible, a face that was inhuman save for the two eyes that stared at her.

For a moment she glimpsed it and then a wave of blackness blotted out everything, and she fainted.

22

The Girl in the Wood

Jim read the letter through a second time and smiled grimly. It was a sign of weakness on his adversary's part to have sent that, it showed fear. Queer Face was afraid of him. He was so afraid of him that he had tried twice to get him out of the way and having failed, had resorted to this unoriginal method of sending him a warning. Folding the note up, he put it back in its envelope and glanced at the postmark. It had been posted in Little Siltley.

He shrugged his shoulders and slipped the letter into his pocket. If Queer Face was under the impression that he was going to frighten him away in this rather hackneyed manner, he was mistaken.

He went in search of Freddy Kemp, but the journalist was not in, although lunch was already being laid in the coffee-room.

'Mr. Kemp has gone for a walk,' said Joyce in answer to his inquiry. 'He took some sandwiches with him and said he wouldn't be back till teatime.'

Jim ate his lunch alone. If the truth must be told, he was rather glad of the solitude, for he had a lot to think about. When the meal was over he went up to his room, washed, and decided to while away the remainder of the afternoon with a stroll round the neighbourhood. He was one of those people who could think better when his brain was stimulated by a little gentle exercise. He bought some cigarettes at the bar on his way out, and turned up towards the High Street.

The afternoon was very quiet and sleepy, one of those lazy afternoons when the country is a joy, and Jim strolled gently along, almost completely contented. He began to wish that there were no such things as crimes and criminals to disturb the soothing peace that surrounded him on every side. And yet, amidst this beauty, murder had stalked abroad, and in the leafy lanes and shaded woods lurked a menace that was like a parasite that gnawed at the heart of a rosebud. Somewhere in these lovely surroundings a callous and unscrupulous man was hatching a plot of which Jim had but the haziest idea. At any moment murder might be enacted again in the same setting.

His thoughts turned to little Arty Smith and the dark-faced man who had occupied the rear seat in the resplendent car. How, exactly, did these two come into the affair, if indeed they came into it at all? Had Captain Freeman come down to see the man who called himself Hillbury on some other business unconnected with Queer Face? Or was he mixed up in the general scheme of things? Jim found no satisfactory answer to this. He had no proof beyond his own conviction that the man Freeman had called on Mr. Hillbury at all, but with the exception of a few scattered cottages Dead Trees was the only house in the direction in which Arty Smith had driven the car, and the fact that he had returned so quickly after picking up his employer showed that Freeman could not have gone very far afield.

He was still conjecturing as to the presence of these two additional factors in the case when the little footpath took a sharp bend, and rounding it he came in sight of a stile, beyond which lay the beginning of a belt of woodland. A movement among the trees caught his eye, and looking up he saw that a girl was coming slowly towards him. At first he thought it was Phyllis Orde, and then he discovered it was a stranger.

She was slim and dark, and moved with an easy, graceful carriage. Jim slowed down in order to give her time to climb the stile before he reached it, but she was sauntering so slowly that they both arrived at the barrier together. She gave him a momentary glance as he stood aside, and Jim thought he had seldom seen anything so lovely. She stepped over the top bar of the stile, and was descending on his side when her foot caught and she stumbled. In trying to save herself she dropped her handbag, which she was carrying under one arm. Jim stooped to pick it up, and as he did so saw two golden initials stamped in the leather, L. A.

It was not until he had handed the girl her bag and she had uttered a polite word of thanks that the significance of those initials occurred to him. L. A. Lesley Allerton, the girl who had signed the hastily scrawled note that had been the means of bringing him into this strange business.

She had moved on, and was walking away from him before he had recovered from the shock of the discovery. It couldn't possibly be anything more than coincidence; probably the letters on the bag stood for quite a different name, and yet . . .

Acting on an impulse he followed her quickly.

'Excuse me,' he said as he overtook her, 'but is your name Allerton, Lesley Allerton?'

She stopped and looked at him coldly, her pencilled brows drawn down into a frown over her grey eyes.

'It is,' she said. 'Why?'

He was momentarily staggered.

'Because — because — ' He grew a little incoherent and then recovered himself. 'You're the girl who wrote that message,' he said.

The eyebrows went up in surprise.

'Message?' she repeated, and shook her head, 'I don't know what you're talking about.'

'Didn't you throw a message over the wall at Dead Trees?' he said rapidly, 'saying that you were being kept a prisoner, and that you were in danger — '

She gave him a blank stare.

'I think you must have made a mistake,' she said coolly. 'I know nothing about Dead Trees, or any message.'

'But,' stammered Jim, completely bewildered, 'your name is Lesley Allerton?'

'Oh, yes, my name is Lesley Allerton,' she answered.

'And you live round here?' he went on eagerly.

Her lips compressed.

'Really, I don't know what that has to do with you,' she retorted. 'Either you're mad, or this is just an excuse to speak to me. In either case I don't wish to know you.'

She turned and walked quickly away, leaving Jim staring after her, his mind a chaos of bewildered thoughts.

As she vanished round the bend of the little footpath he felt for his cigarettes, lighted one, and going back to the stile perched himself on it and smoked thoughtfully. It was impossible that there could be two Lesley Allertons in Little Siltley, and yet this girl, while admitting that her name was Lesley Allerton, had denied all knowledge of the message and Dead Trees.

During his short life Jim had experienced a good many shocks but none quite so devastating as this one. The girl must be lying, yet so far as he could see there was no reason why she should. If she was the same Lesley Allerton who had been kept a prisoner at the Hillburys', why should she try and keep the fact a secret? She was obviously free and her own mistress, and the natural thing, in the circumstances, would have been to have gone to the police and laid information against the fat man who had kept her incarcerated in that ugly and unpleasant house. But apparently she not only had no wish to make the matter public, but was prepared to lie in order to shield Hillbury from the results of his lawlessness.

Jim blew a cloud of blue smoke into the air and watched it slowly disperse. It was beyond him, and he frankly admitted it. Finishing his cigarette he continued his walk, reaching the Load of Hay in time for tea, a tired and puzzled man.

Throughout the evening he pondered over that chance meeting by the stile, and he was so obviously preoccupied that Freddy Kemp eventually gave up trying to talk to him and went out to find Phyllis Orde. When he came back, twenty minutes later, Jim found that a fresh complication had been added to the burden he was already grappling with, for he learned from the distracted journalist that the girl had not returned to Mrs. Jillider's cottage since she had left it in the early part of that afternoon.

23

The Thing In the Room

Phyllis Orde's first conscious sensation as she came out of the black mist of her faint was one of acute physical discomfort. Every bone in her body ached, and there was a dull pain at her wrists and ankles. For some time her brain was still rather hazy, and it was several minutes before she was able to discover the reason for these unpleasantnesses, and then she found that the aches in her body were caused by the hard floor on which she was lying, and the soreness of her ankles and wrists was due to them being tightly bound with thin cord.

She was in a small, square room that was lighted by a narrow oblong window set high up near the ceiling. The floor was carpetless and there was no furniture, and from the fact that there was a large cupboard in one corner and a coat rack screwed in the wall she concluded that it was some kind of a lobby.

As memory came flooding back to her she reasoned that she was somewhere inside Lady's Manor. Curiously enough, she felt no fear, only an intense curiosity as to what these people would do with her. Obviously they had no intention of letting her go; the fact that they had taken the precaution of tying her up while she was unconscious proved that.

She regretted now the sudden impulse that had made her come to this place, and wondered how soon it would be before Jim and Freddy discovered her absence. Probably it would be a long time, and even when they did it was unlikely they would guess where she was. She had started out with the intention of getting into conversation with one of Mr. Hillbury's bodyguards, and they would naturally conclude when she didn't come back that she had succeeded in her purpose. When time went on, and they realised that something had happened to her, they would never connect it with the inhabitants of Lady's Manor, but would jump to the natural conclusion that she had fallen foul of the people in Dead Trees. It was unlikely that she could expect any help, therefore, from her two friends.

In the midst of these thoughts she heard a door bang, followed by the sound of quick, light footsteps. The footsteps were those of a woman unmistakably and she was wondering who this could be when she heard the rather husky voice of the white-faced man speaking.

'Did you enjoy your walk, darling?' he said.

'Yes, thanks,' came the reply, the low voice of a girl. 'I had an adventure though. I met that man Brent.'

Phil heard the man utter an exclamation, and then the girl said something in such a low tone that although she strained her ears she couldn't catch a word.

'You'll have to be careful,' said the man's voice again. 'Not that you're likely to meet him again. We're leaving here early in the morning.'

'He didn't look very desperate,' replied the girl. 'In fact, to be quite candid, I thought he was rather nice, not a bit like a criminal.'

The man's reply was inaudible, and they both moved away and Phyllis Orde heard nothing more, but the little she had heard gave her a lot to think about. Who was this girl who had met Jim Brent, and why was she under the impression that he was a crook? Apparently because she had been told so by the white-faced man. So they were clearing out in the morning, were they? That meant that the reason for their presence was over, or would be over that night. Something then must have happened to advance their plans, for when she had heard them talking earlier they had been discussing something that was to take place on the following night. Probably it was her presence that had caused the alteration.

She frowned. If she could only get into communication with Jim and Freddy and warn them that these people were on the point of clearing out! But that seemed impossible. She was completely helpless, and could move neither hand nor foot. The cord had been tied so tightly that it cut into her flesh; and although she strained her wrists apart to try and loosen them, it had no effect.

The time passed slowly and nobody came near her. Occasionally she heard movements in the house, but otherwise it was very quiet. By degrees the oblong of window grew less bright. The sunlight outside was fading and being replaced by the dusk of evening. She could not tell what the time was, for her hands had been tied behind her back and it was impossible to see her wristwatch, but from the light she judged that it must be somewhere in the region of nine o'clock. Her mouth and throat were dry, and she would have given anything for a cup of tea.

It was completely dark outside when the hitherto silent house awoke to sounds of bustling activity. Hurried footsteps passed and re-passed the door, and she heard the whispering of voices. The queer faced man spoke to somebody, and she caught a word or two here and there.

'The car will be waiting . . . Four o'clock . . . By that time . . . Finish with Gleeson . . . '

The deeper tones of Patterson-Willis replied.

'What are you doing with that girl, and the other?'

'Leaving them,' answered the other. 'By the time they are found we shall be well away.' He stopped abruptly with a cautious 'Sh-s-sh! My daughter'; and the girl's voice that had spoken earlier reached Phil's ears.

'Are you coming back here for me, father?' she asked.

'No.'

The voice of the queer faced man was clearer now, and Phil concluded that he must be standing immediately outside the door.

'We shall meet you at the car; there's no point in coming back here, Lesley!'

Lesley! Phil stifled an exclamation.

So this girl was the girl who had been imprisoned in Dead Trees. A thrill of excitement ran through her. If only she were free and could get to Jim and Freddy! She strained and tugged at her bonds till she winced with the pain, but there were no signs of slackening, and she stopped at last exhausted.

The voices and movements outside her

door had ceased, and for some time there was silence again. Then she heard the sound of shuffling feet and panting breath, accompanied by a queer dragging sound. There was the rasp of a key in the lock, and by the sudden blast of cold air that blew in on her she guessed the door of the lobby had been opened.

'Quick!' panted the voice of the queer faced man — 'before Lesley comes back.'

Something was thrust into the room and fell near her and then the door was closed and the key once more turned. Something soft and bulky lay across her feet, and twisting over on her side away from it she felt about with her fingers. At first she could feel nothing, for her bound wrists restricted her movements and then groping she touched something cold and soft and but for the gag about her mouth would have screamed aloud for the thing her fingers had come in contact with was the cold flesh of a human face.

24

Night at Dead Trees

The trees that grew so thickly in the vicinity of Mr. Hillbury's fortress-like house whispered together eerily as their leaves were stirred by the breeze, which had come up with nightfall.

In the clear sky a sickle moon hung low, a rind of silver that gave such little light that it seemed by contrast to add to the general darkness.

George Cusher, a cigarette in his mouth and his hands in his pockets, patrolled slowly up the weed-grown drive, completed a circle of the house, and met the taciturn Sam who had just done a round of the grounds.

'No sign of anyone,' grunted Cusher, and it was more a question than a statement.

Sam Clark shook his head.

'No,' he growled. 'I'm getting a bit sick

of this job, George. Shan't be sorry to see a bit of life and gaiety. This place gives me the creeps, particularly after what happened to Dan.'

'You don't want to go talking about that,' said Cusher, glancing uneasily over his shoulder. 'I'm as much fed up as you are, but the pay's good, and we shall touch for a nice little wad when the job's over.'

'If we don't get our throats cut,' said the pessimistic Sam. 'See here, George, what's the old beggar afraid of?'

Mr. Cusher shrugged his shoulders.

'Ask me,' he replied. ''E pitched me some yarn about this white-faced fellow bein' an old associate of his who had a grievance, but you can take it from me that it's somethin' more than that. It's my opinion the old blighter's done 'im a bad turn, and a pretty low down one, too.'

'H'm,' grunted Sam. 'Well, I think we shall be darned lucky if we get out of this with a whole skin, and even then we shall probably be pinched,' he added darkly.

'You're a nice, happy sort of chap, ain't yer!' snarled Cusher. 'Always lookin' on the bright side of things, I don't think!'

'Well, the police are pretty suspicious,' argued his companion. 'Look at the way they searched the place for that gal.'

'Yes, and they found a hell of a lot, didn't they?' retorted Cusher.

'Whether they found anything or not,' said Mr. Clark, 'I'll bet they haven't given up hope. Look at that bit of skirt what was waitin' outside this afternoon! She tried 'er 'ardest to get me into conversation, and I'll bet she wasn't as innocent as she looked. And then there was that fellow that called this mornin', Captain Freedman, or whatever 'is name was — '

'Freeman,' supplied Cusher. ''E hasn't anythin' to do with the police, 'e was a friend of the old man's.'

''E didn't look very friendly to me,' grunted the other. ' 'E 'ad a face on 'im when 'e went away that was as ugly as sin.'

'The old man wouldn't see 'im,' said Cusher. 'That's what annoyed 'im.'

'Well, I'll be glad when we get back to London anyway,' grumbled Sam. 'I wasn't cut out for a country life.'

They chatted for a few moments longer and then parted to continue their patrol of the grounds. Mr. Cusher began to make a circuit of the high brick wall, and presently arrived at that portion where Lesley Allerton, in a moment when she was unguarded, had succeeded in throwing over the message which had brought Jim Brent and Superintendent Laker to the house. And on the other side of that wall, unknown to the guardian within, Mr. Arty Smith sat at the wheel of the resplendent car, which Jim had so unjustly referred to as a bandwagon, and talked in low tones to his dark-faced employer.

'It's half past twelve now,' whispered Captain Freeman. 'We'd better leave it till one, the old devil ought to be asleep by then.'

Mr. Smith nodded.

'D'you think you can do it?' went on the other anxiously.

'Easy as kiss yer 'and,' answered the little man. 'It's a pity you couldn't get in, though, to 'ave a dekker at the place.'

'The old so-and-so wouldn't see me,'

grunted his companion. 'Sent a tough looking guy to tell me he was busy and wasn't seeing anyone, then or any time. Anyway, once we're inside we'll make him show us the lay of the land himself. I've got something here that ought to persuade him to talk.'

He patted his hip pocket.

'You want to be careful with that,' muttered Mr. Smith anxiously. 'I don't 'old with carrying them things myself, Never did. If you're caught with a gun it means — '

'We're not going to be caught, with or without a gun,' snapped Captain Freeman impatiently. 'Gleeson daren't raise the alarm, that's the beauty of this job. How long do you think it will take you to open that wicket?'

'About one second,' said Arty Smith extravagantly. 'The lock they've got on that gate ain't a protection, it's an invitation.'

'There's probably some kind of alarm,' warned the other.

'Sure there is,' said Mr. Smith, who was a great patron of gangster films in his leisure moments. 'But that doesn't mean anything in my young life.'

They lapsed into silence, and while they waited for the minute hand of Captain Freeman's wristwatch to turn slowly towards one, Mr. Hillbury, unaware of their existence so near to his abode, prepared to retire for the night.

He undressed slowly by the light of a candle, his shaking hands fumbling with the fastening of his collar, for that evening he had consumed a large amount of the courage that is to be found in a bottle.

His wife, who occupied a room on the floor above, had long since gone to bed, and the house was very silent and still save for those queer noises that are heard in every house after nightfall.

But tonight the fat man was unperturbed by the creaks and cracks that every now and again shattered the stillness. There had been nights when they had sent him white-faced and shivering with fear to the door of his room to peer out into the darkened corridor fearfully, his imagination conjuring up a stealthy step ascending the stair. But the whisky he had consumed had dulled his senses and filled him with a spurious contempt for the man he feared. Harry couldn't get at him, not here in this closely guarded house, with its high wall, reinforced locks and electric alarms. He was as safe as if he was shut up in a vault at the Bank of England.

He chuckled as he slid his flabby limbs into a suit of silk pyjamas. Lew Gleeson had been too clever. Harry might think he was a fool, but for all his talk he'd beaten him, and he'd continue to beat him. He'd have to get up very early to get the better of Lew Gleeson.

He tumbled into the protesting bed, blew out the candle, and pulled the clothes round his fat shoulders. He had snuggled his head comfortably down into the pillow when he remembered that he had forgotten to lock the door. Oh, well, it didn't matter; nobody would be able to get past those two fellows who would patrol the grounds, faithful and watchful, until dawn. He was far too tired and comfortable to move, and as the thought ran out of his mind he fell asleep . . .

Almost instantly it seemed he was awake, his heart bumping fearfully and a cold sweat on his forehead. He had no idea what had awakened him, for he had heard no sound, but something had penetrated his consciousness and dragged him terror-stricken back to sensibility. He sat up, staring with starting eyes at the closed door, and as he looked a strangled cry rose from his dry throat, for the door was slowly opening.

The sliver of moon had risen high in the sky, and its reflected light was sufficient to fill the bedroom with a ghostly radiance Slowly, noiselessly, the door opened wider, and the fat man, paralysed with fear, could only watch it, motionless.

In, out of the darkness of the passage outside, came a figure. A tall, thin figure. A husky voice broke the silence. A voice that was low and almost caressing.

'I've come for you, Lew,' it said.

The shivering man in the bed caught a glimpse of the bloated, puffy white face, and knew that his end was at hand.

25

The Panic of Arty Smith

The three men who sat in the coffee-room in the Load of Hay looked weary and dispirited. Superintendent Laker, his lean face the picture of gloom, stared at his empty coffee cup and played with an unlighted cigarette. Jim, his brows drawn together in a frown, sat opposite him, and Freddy Kemp, his big bulk wedged uncomfortably in a Windsor chair, looked from one to the other, his usually florid face pale and haggard.

When they had discovered that Phyllis Orde had gone out that afternoon and had not returned, they had set out to try and find her. For nearly two hours they had patrolled the lanes and roads in the vicinity, each taking a different direction and arranging to meet later at the inn, but without result. There had been no sign of the girl, but eventually Jim had gone down to the police station and consulted the Superintendent. He had suggested that Laker should go at once to Dead Trees and make inquiries, but that official had been dubious.

'We've no proof that these people have got anything to do with Miss Orde's absence,' he argued, not unreasonably, 'and after the result of the previous search I daren't do it, Mr. Brent. The Chief Constable'd have me on the carpet.

'Oh, yes, I know you told me that the young lady was going to try and get into conversation with one of those fellows, but we've no evidence that she did. In fact, we've no evidence at all that she's staying away except of her own accord, and it's no good my turning out the police to look for her and then discovering that she's gone into the neighbouring town to the pictures.'

There was a lot of truth in what he said, and Jim, although he was convinced that something had happened to the girl, was forced to see his point of view. They had gone back to the inn and waited in the faint hope that the girl would come back. At half-past eleven, when there was still no sign of her, Freddy went down to Mrs. Jillider's to inquire if she had returned, but the anxious landlady had no news, and returning to Jim he found that Laker had dropped in on his way home to learn if anything had been heard of her.

'No,' growled Freddy. 'Nothing. And it's my belief nothing ever will unless we do something quickly. She's fallen foul of one of those brutes at Dead Trees, you mark my words, and if she isn't back by twelve o'clock I'm going up to the house myself.'

'You won't do any good by doing that, Freddy,' said Jim quietly. 'Even if they've got her there, they're not likely to tell you.'

'If I get my hands on one of those bruisers,' said the reporter, clenching his huge fist grimly, 'I'll damn soon make him tell me the truth.'

He was worried and irritable, but after much argument Laker and Jim between them succeeded in dissuading him from a course that could not have done any good.

'Well, what can we do?' he demanded.

'It's all very well for you to sit there and say it's no good my going up to the place, but we must do something. We can't just say, 'Oh, Phil's disappeared', and leave it at that.'

'Nobody's going to leave it at that,' said Jim, 'but it's a difficult situation. As Laker says, we can't get another search warrant. We haven't sufficient grounds to get it on, and if we go up to Dead Trees to make inquiries, all they'll say is that they don't know anything about the girl and have never seen her.'

'That's true, Mr. Brent,' agreed the Superintendent.

'Well, perhaps you'll suggest an alternative course!' snarled Freddy, and flung himself into a chair as Joyce entered with coffee which they had previously ordered.

They drank it in gloomy silence, and Laker was in the act of lighting the cigarette he had been fiddling about with so long when Jim looked up suddenly and spoke.

'There's only one thing to do,' he said, 'and that's for me to go up to Dead Trees and see if I can learn anything.'

'I thought you said it was useless?' grunted Freddy, 'When — '

'I said it was useless making inquiries,' broke in Jim, 'and I still say so. But I'm not suggesting that I should go up and ring the bell, I'm suggesting that I should do as I did before.'

'You mean, climb the wall?' said the reporter and Jim nodded.

Laker pursed his lips doubtfully.

'It's illegal, you know, Mr. Brent,' he warned.

'So is everything at Dead Trees,' retorted Jim. 'It's the only way, Laker, you must see that. I'm certain that Miss Orde has aroused these people's suspicions and has been kidnapped. So far as I'm concerned, I haven't any doubt that she's in the house at the moment.'

'And for all we know, in danger of her life,' put in Freddy, rising to his feet and pacing the room restlessly. 'I think your idea's a good one, old man. I'll come with you.'

But Jim shook his head.

'No good doing that, old man,' he answered. 'It will be difficult enough for me to get into the place unobserved, but if there were two of us we're almost certain to the discovered. The grounds are riddled with alarm and trip wires, and those fellows are always on duty. I'm going to have all my work cut out to get in at all, but I'm going to do it.'

'When are you going?' asked Kemp. 'Now?'

Again Jim shook his head.

'No; we'll leave it until about one, I think,' he said. 'The later it is the better. By that time everybody except the guard will be asleep.'

'Well, I wish you'd let me come with you,' grunted the reporter. 'I don't like the idea of your going into this place on your own. At any rate, I can come as far as the wall, then if you get into any kind of trouble you can give a shout.'

'Yes, you can do that,' agreed Jim.

'And I'll come with you,' said Laker, to his surprise. 'The whole thing's most irregular, Mr. Brent, and having said that, I'm not going to be left out of it.'

'Good for you!' cried Freddy, and gave the lean man a grateful glance.

'Well, I can't do much officially,' said the Superintendent with a wry smile, 'so the least I can do is to help unofficially.'

'You're a sport, Laker,' said Jim. 'We'll leave here at ten to one.'

The Superintendent hoisted his lean form out of the chair.

'I'll slip along home and have my supper and then come back,' he said, and with a nod left them.

Just after he had gone they heard the landlady going round locking up, and Jim called her into the coffee-room.

'My friend and I will be going out just before one,' he explained, 'so if you hear anyone moving about you'll know that it's us.'

Mrs. Lanning looked a little surprised.

'Then I'd better leave the chain and bolt off the front door, sir,' she said.

'Yes, thank you,' answered Jim.

The landlady hesitated for a moment, and then fumbling in the pockets of her spotless apron she produced a key.

'You'd better have this too, sir,' she remarked, 'otherwise you won't be able to get in.'

Jim, who had been contemplating using the lean-to shed of his bedroom window as a means of ingress on his return, thanked her and took the key. The landlady wished them good night and departed, and they settled down to wait, with what patience they could, until it was time for them to start on their expedition. At twenty minutes to one they heard a step outside, followed by a short tap at the door, and going out into the hall Jim admitted Laker.

A clock in the village was just striking one as the three of them crept softly out of the Load of Hay and turned in the direction of the rise leading up to Dead Trees. They walked quickly and in silence, and they were half way up the slope when Jim's quick ears heard a sound ahead of them, the sound of running footsteps coming towards them. With a muttered word to his companions he stopped and listened. The footsteps grew louder, and presently in the pale light of the new moon he was able to make out a figure running wildly down the road. It was zig-zagging from side to side like someone who was drunk, and as it drew nearer he saw that it was the figure of a man. Sobbing breath came to his ears, and then suddenly the runner saw them and stopped, swaying in the middle of the roadway,

Jim hurried forward, and then as he caught sight of the man's face he uttered an exclamation.

'Why, it's Arty Smith!' he exclaimed.

The man stared at him in terror, and then as he saw who it was an expression of relief crossed his face.

'Mr. Brent, for Gawd's sake,' he muttered huskily, and then, before Jim could catch him he crumpled up and fell a sprawling heap at his feet.

Jim looked at his hand where it had touched the other's coat sleeve. It was red with blood.

26

Queer Face

The menacing figure with that dreadful face came further into the room, and now the horrified man on the bed could see that it held in one hand a long-barrelled automatic.

'We meet again, Lew,' said the soft voice. 'What have you to say?'

Mr. Hillbury, his plump hands clutching feverishly at the collar of his pyjama jacket, could say nothing. His throat was dry and parched with the fear that consumed him. He could only stare dumbly at the terrifying shape, his breath hissing from his open mouth in little short, irregular gasps.

'Get up,' said Queer Face, and the fat man hastened to obey the order.

He dragged his trembling limbs from the bed and tried to stand, but his shaking knees offered no support and he had to clutch the rail to prevent himself falling.

'My appearance has given you a shock,' said Queer Face and uttered a soft, throaty chuckle. 'And yet, after what I told you on the telephone, you should have been prepared to see me. I told you that in spite of your precautions I should come when I liked, and here I am.'

Mr. Hillbury licked his dry lips and swallowed twice painfully, but the words he essayed to utter stuck in his throat and only a faint, gurgling rattle came.

'Put on your dressing gown,' said the man by the door, 'and don't hope that your guards will help you. They have been accounted for.'

Hillbury reached for his dressing gown and dragged it round his shivering form. He looked like a horrible, bloated jellyfish as he stood there glaring at his enemy.

'You know what I've come for, Lew,' went on Queer Face, and Mr. Hillbury, by a supreme effort succeeded in finding his voice, or a voice, for when he spoke it was totally unlike his own. 'Yes, yes, of course, Harry,' he almost croaked, 'and you shall have it. You shall have it, Harry. You know I wouldn't do you down, old man. Didn't I say when you telephoned me that if we got together and had a little chat everything would be all right! Didn't I say so?'

The other eyed him. His eyes in the dead whiteness of that shapeless face glowing like coals.

'You haven't even got the redeeming virtue of courage,' he said contemptuously. 'I trusted you, Lew, and you let me down. You thought I'd never recover from that accident, didn't you? You thought I'd die in the hospital in Germany! You hoped I would, so that the stuff you had stolen from me might, remain your property without any trouble.'

'I thought you were dead, Harry,' said the fat man eagerly. 'I swear I did. When I heard of the train accident I sent a man to make enquiries, he told me you had died in hospital.'

'You lie,' said Queer Face, coldly and unemotionally. 'When you learned of the accident and found how badly I had been injured you saw a chance of keeping the jewels which I had given you for disposal for yourself. You ignored my letters, refused to see my daughter, and when you discovered that I had not died, as you hoped, but had recovered, you fled to this house in a panic. You knew that I should become aware of your perfidy and you were afraid, afraid of the scarred and injured man you had double-crossed. And you had cause to fear, Lew.'

'No, no,' broke in the shaking man he was addressing. 'You've got me wrong, Harry.'

'It's useless lying,' snarled Queer Face. 'You kidnapped my daughter hoping to hold her as a hostage in case I should find you knowing that she's the only thing I care about in the world, but your plan availed you nothing. When, to hoodwink the police who had obtained a warrant to search this house, you lowered Lesley into the well as a hiding place you delivered her into my hands. You have no hostage to save you now, Lew.'

The fat man's flabby face was bedewed with perspiration, and the blood had receded from his cheeks, leaving them a pallid grey. In his heart he knew that he could expect no mercy from the man before him, and his craven spirit quaked.

'Be reasonable, Harry,' he whimpered 'Perhaps I have been silly, but everyone's liable to make mistakes, and I'll do anything you like to make reparation.'

Queer Face uttered a short laugh.

'You'll make reparation all right, Lew,' he said meaningfully. 'Now tell me, where are the diamonds you stole, are they intact?'

'Yes, every one of them,' quavered Mr. Hillbury. 'Every one of them, Harry. I didn't dispose of a single stone.'

'Because you couldn't,' interrupted the other sharply. 'To do so you would have had to take them to the Continent yourself and you were afraid to leave your stronghold. Where have you got them?'

'I'll show you.' The fat man made a movement towards the door.

'Don't try any tricks,' warned Queer Face and the other uttered a little gasp as he felt the hard muzzle of the automatic grind into his back. 'At the first sign of any treachery I shall shoot.'

The fat man stumbled along the passage to the head of the stairs, and in the darkness with the other close behind him and the pistol still touching his spine, groped his way down to the hall. He led the way to the small study-like room in which he had interviewed Laker and Jim on the night of Dan Killick's murder and taking a key from his dressing gown pocket, unlocked the door. With unsteady steps he went over to the fireplace, knelt on the rug and with trembling hands pulled at one of the bricks forming the hearth. After some little trouble he succeeded in lifting it out and thrust his hand into the hole revealed. Feeling about with his stubby fingers he produced a wash-leather bag and laid it on the floor beside him. Six in all he produced and stood them beside the first.

'That's the lot,' he muttered huskily, 'and there isn't a single stone missing.'

'There had better not be,' said Queer Face. 'Open them and turn them out on the table.'

The fat man obeyed and presently, as he emptied bag after bag, there grew on the polished surface of the table a mountain of shimmering light. There were diamonds of all sizes, every one of which had been removed from its setting, diamonds, the description of which had been circulated throughout the country. When the last bag had been emptied Queer Face surveyed the pile and his eyes gleamed.

'Mine, Lew,' he muttered. 'All mine. A fortune to compensate me for this.' He raised his left hand and touched the dreadful, mutilated face that had resulted from that tragic train accident. For nearly a minute he stared in silence at the glittering heap, and then he turned towards the grovelling figure of the fat man. 'Put them back in the bag,' he ordered.

'You're going to be sensible, Harry, aren't you?' pleaded the fat man. 'Take this stuff and let bygones be bygones. It's no good nursing an injury and you haven't lost anything.'

'If you offered me all the money in the world, Lew,' broke in Queer Face coldly, 'you couldn't turn me from my purpose.

For two and a half years I've waited for this moment. At night I've lain awake and thought of it.'

'I can't do more than give up the stuff, Harry,' whined Mr. Hillbury. 'Surely you're satisfied with that? I've suffered too, I've never known a moment's peace . . .'

'Since you knew I was alive,' finished the other. 'No, I don't suppose you have, Lew. I'll bet you've lived in a state of terror, quaking for your wretched skin, and you had cause, but we'll talk about that presently. In the meanwhile, pack those diamonds away and give them to me.'

With almost pathetic eagerness the fat man hastened to obey the order. Scooping up the glittering gems in his fat fingers he allowed them to trickle back into the wash-leather bags and he had just filled the sixth when a voice from the doorway caused them both to swing round.

'That's saved me a lot of trouble,' it said pleasantly. 'Put up your hands, Gleeson, and drop that pistol, you, whoever you are.'

The dark-faced, smiling man who stood in the doorway made a menacing gesture with the weapon he held in his right hand.

'Flash Fred!' gasped Mr. Hillbury as his fat arms went up towards the ceiling.

'Yes, Flash Fred,' said Captain Freeman pleasantly. 'You wouldn't see me when I called before, would you, Gleeson? Well, perhaps this time I've dropped in at a more opportune moment.' Without turning his head he addressed the little man who was standing behind him. 'Pick up those bags, Arty.'

The little man who was hovering in the background behind him came forward eagerly. For a fraction of a second as he moved the eyes of Captain Freeman wavered, and in that second Queer Face acted. The pistol in his hand jerked up, there was a report and the man by the door staggered. A ludicrous expression of dismay crossed his face, then his knees gave way under him and he slithered gently to the floor. The man who had shot him darted forward and wrenched the pistol from his nerveless hand.

'Now,' he said, facing the frightened Arty Smith and the cringing Hillbury, 'leave those diamonds alone or I'll treat you the same as your friend.'

27

Exit Lew Gleeson

Arty Smith moved back from the table and crouched against the wall, his little eyes round with fear. Ignoring him, Queer Face looked at Hillbury. 'Give me those bags and look sharp about it,' he said. The fat man clawed the little wash-leather bags together in his trembling hands and brought them over to him. 'Put them in my pocket,' ordered the other, and the man called Lew obeyed.

Arty Smith licked his dry lips and watched in silence. His companion, the man who called himself Captain Freeman, was dead, one glance at his face told him that, and he wondered what this dreadful man with the distorted visage was going to do to him. Lew Gleeson, alias Hillbury, was wondering the same thing, although it was not Mr. Smith's fate that concerned him but his own.

'What about this fellow, Harry?' he asked in a conciliatory tone, jerking his head towards the shivering Arty Smith. 'What are you going to do with him?'

'I'll attend to him presently,' answered Queer Face. 'It's you I'm concerned with at the moment.'

His voice was hard and emotionless, but the tone of it sent a cold shiver down the fat man's spine.

'You wouldn't do anything to me, Harry, would you?' he muttered hoarsely. 'After all, we've been friends, why can't we be friends again?'

'Because it's difficult to be friendly with a dead man,' snarled the other, 'and that's what you'll be before I leave here.'

Lew Gleeson uttered a gasp and the terror of his face made it horrible to look upon.

'Won't you listen to reason, Harry,' he began, and stopped as a sound reached him from the silent house — the sound of a footstep descending the stairs.

Queer Face heard it too and drew to the side of the doorway.

'Is anything the matter, Lew?' called

the woman's voice.

Queer Face stepped quickly to the fat man's side.

'Tell her to go back to bed,' he hissed in his ear. 'Tell her there's nothing the matter.'

'There's nothing the matter, Myra,' said Gleeson striving to keep his voice from trembling. 'Nothing at all, go back to bed.'

But in spite of his reassurance the woman seemed unconvinced.

'What was that noise?' she asked. 'It sounded like a shot.'

'I — I knocked over a chair,' answered her husband. 'Don't make a fuss, Myra, go back to bed.'

There was a pause and then she said:

'Why are you up at this hour?'

He passed his tongue over his dry lips.

'I couldn't sleep. I came down to get some cigarettes.'

'All right,' she answered, 'but if you're going to moon about all night for the Lord's sake do it quietly. I want some sleep if you don't.'

They heard her footsteps going back up

the stairs and presently the sound of a closing door. A little hissing breath of relief came from the lips of the white-faced man.

'It's lucky for her she was satisfied,' he muttered, and at that instant, Arty, who during their pre-occupation had been edging his way stealthily nearer the door, made a dash for the exit.

Springing over the prone figure of the dead man he disappeared into the darkness of the passage, before Queer Face could do anything to stop his unexpected movement. The man uttered an oath and was following him when there came the sound of voices followed by a little, thin scream.

'The fool's ran into Nat and Hansard,' muttered Queer Face. 'They'll look after him.' He glanced at the perspiring Gleeson. 'Now I'll attend to you, Lew,' he said.

His voice had changed, and something in its tone warned the fat man that the time had come. The small amount of self-control he still possessed deserted him.

'Harry, have mercy!' he croaked. 'You've got the diamonds, you've got everything. Don't bear malice, old man . . . '

Muttering incoherently, pleadingly, he stumbled forward and dropping to his knees grovelled at the feet of the inexorable figure that stood looking down at him, his shapeless lips twisted into a contemptuous smile.

'You're a contemptible thing, Lew,' he said above the other's whimpered pleading. 'A contemptible thing. You always were! Get up, and meet your fate like a man. If you'd stolen the diamonds and faced it out I might have admired you, although it would have been a filthy trick, but you didn't. You crawled away to this hole like a rat, and while you thought you were safe you were brave enough. Nothing you can say or do will alter me. You've got to take what's coming to you.' He pocketed his pistol and, stooping, gripped the fat man by the collar of his dressing gown. With a jerk he hauled him to his feet. 'The time has come. Lew,' he said, and a little moaning sob of terror escaped Gleeson as he saw the knife that had appeared in the other's hand.

'Harry! For God's sake!' he gasped

huskily, and it was the last thing he ever said.

The thin blade flashed in the light and with a little choking sound Lew Gleeson collapsed to the floor, an obscene heap of quivering flesh, the red of his blood adding to the many colours of his gaudy dressing gown. For a moment the body twitched spasmodically and then lay still. Queer Face looked at it, took a handkerchief from his pocket and wiped his hand. His work was finished, there was nothing left for him to do but to go, back through the passage that communicated with Lady's Manor, and by the time daylight came he would be miles away on the threshold of the new life he had planned. A life of ease and comfort abroad in the company of the daughter he loved.

Ruthless, regardless of human life, Lesley Allerton was the one human spot in this man's queer nature. He loved his daughter with a devotion that few men could have equalled. Perhaps if her mother had not died at her birth his life might have been different, but the love he had given the mother had been transferred to the child, augmented a thousandfold. She knew nothing of his real character, was unaware that he was a jewel thief and a murderer. She was under the impression that he was connected with the secret service, and this illusion he had carefully fostered, explaining away many things by its aid.

He replaced his handkerchief in his pocket and patted the bulges made by the diamonds. There was a man in Antwerp who would pay him good American currency for those stones. There would be money in plenty to keep himself and Lesley in luxury. He took a last look at the obese mountain of flesh that had been Lew Gleeson and turning, passed out of the death room into the darkness of the passage.

He made his way cautiously along in the direction of the kitchens. These remained practically unaltered from the time the house had been built. The walls and flooring were of solid stone and the ceiling supported on thick rafters. Near the dresser a feeble electric light burned dimly and revealed an oblong opening in one of the thick walls. This was the entrance to the passage, which communicated with Lady's Manor, and along which, in the old days, many a dainty foot had stolen in the silence of the night.

The old well in the grounds formed an air shaft to this passage, and it was while on a voyage of exploration that he had discovered his daughter. At first he had been under the impression that Gleeson had killed her, but on cutting her down he thankfully discovered that she was alive and well.

He crossed the big kitchen towards the irregular shaped opening and was two yards from it when he heard a sound from within, and stopped. The head and shoulders of a man appeared, rising out of the gloom as he ascended the moss-covered steps that led downwards.

'Hansard,' began Queer Face, and broke off abruptly, his hand flying to his pocket, for as the man came into the light he saw that it was not Hansard, but the real Patterson-Willis, and behind him he caught sight of the pale face of Phyllis Orde.

28

Jim Pays a Debt

With a snarl of rage Queer Face whipped his pistol from his pocket and covered them.

'Come out,' he ordered, 'quick, and put up your hands.'

They emerged from the secret entrance blinking, into the light.

'Put up your hands,' snapped Queer Face again, 'and look sharp.'

His brain was working rapidly. Somehow or other these two had got free and he must cope with the unexpected situation.

'Get over there against the wall,' he said, motioning with the muzzle of the automatic, and in silence they obeyed. 'If you move so much as an eyelid, I'll shoot.'

Rapidly he had made his plan. Once he could reach the shelter of the secret passage and close the heavy stone door he would be safe. It could only be opened from inside. He began to back towards the opening, and he had nearly reached it when there came a rush of steps, the kitchen door was flung open and Jim Brent appeared on the threshold followed by Freddy Kemp and Superintendent Laker.

Queer Face muttered an oath and leaped for the oblong hole in the wall. He reached it and tried to close the heavy door, but even as it swung to Jim was across the kitchen and with his shoulder thrust it back. Queer Face levelled his automatic and fired point blank at the young Inspector, but even as his finger pressed the trigger his foot slipped on the slime-covered steps and the bullet went wide, bedding itself in one of the beams of the kitchen ceiling. He tried desperately to save himself from falling, staggered, and went slithering down the steps into the passage below. In falling he struck his elbow sharply and the pistol fell clattering from his nerveless fingers. He landed with a thud that almost winded him, but beyond a few bruises he was unhurt, and picking himself up began to run along the dark and uneven passage. He heard the sound of footsteps behind him and guessed that Jim was following.

The passage sloped downwards steeply and twice he stumbled and almost fell and the footsteps of his pursuer were gaining. Panting heavily, for he was out of condition, Queer Face stumbled on, exerting every ounce of strength, and then, as he realised that he could not hope to outdistance the man who was after him, turned at bay. With a snarl like a trapped animal he hurled himself forward as Jim came up with him. A bunched fist caught him a glancing blow on the cheek and he staggered. The next instant he had closed with the young Inspector and, locked together they struggled desperately in the darkness. Each knew that it was a fight for life, and each put forth all his strength. There was no science about it, it was just a savage struggle, with death for the loser. Back and forth they reeled in the fetid atmosphere of that underground tunnel, hands clawing for a stranglehold. Jim felt his adversary reach his throat, but grasping the wrists he tore them away and hurled the snarling man from him. It gave him a second's respite, but only a second, for his opponent recovered his balance and launched himself once more to the attack. They slipped on the greasy surface beneath them and fell, Jim underneath.

With a hissing breath of triumph Queer Face succeeded in getting his hands round the other's throat. Jim felt the deadly pressure increased until the blood in his head sounded like steam hammers, but keeping his wits about him he jerked up his knees sharply. Queer Face gave a gasp of pain and the grip on Jim's throat relaxed. He twisted himself free and lashed out with his right fist. He felt his knuckles connect with flesh, and as the man above him rolled sideways, followed up his advantage. Flinging himself round, he succeeded in pinning the other beneath him, and in that moment the veneer of civilisation was stripped from him. He was a primitive man fighting for his life, fighting to avenge the death of the father he had loved. His fingers closed round the throat of his enemy, and the snarling curses that the other was mouthing changed to a horrible gurgling noise

Jim increased the pressure. Before his eyes fluttered a red mist and only one thought occupied his brain: here at his mercy was the man who had shot his father . . .

All the pent-up anger that he had nursed for years was suddenly released.

The gurgling ceased, and the straining body of his adversary suddenly went limp. Slowly, in case the other might be playing a trick, Jim released his grasp, but there was no movement from the man beneath him. Scrambling to his feet, his breath coming in irregular gulps, he felt with a shaking hand in his pocket, drew out a box of matches, and striking one peered at the prone figure in its feeble glimmer.

One glance at that bloated white face with its staring eyes and protruding tongue told him all he wanted to know.

Queer Face was dead.

29

Afterwards

The *Clarion* carne out with a special edition. It was the only paper that carried the full story of the tragedy at Little Siltley.

Freddy Kemp had excelled himself and even the taciturn Mr. Poppins smiled sourly when in the early hours of the morning he glanced through a copy of the paper, wet from the press.

In the coffee room at the Load of Hay a party of four sat down to a late and much needed breakfast.

'Well,' remarked Freddy, as he helped himself liberally to marmalade, 'I suppose we can all go back to Town now.'

Jim nodded. He was silent and rather thoughtful, and the reason for this seriousness was the girl, whose disillusionment had been very hard to witness.

It was Phyllis Orde who had told him

about the car waiting for the man who had never returned, and together they had found and broken the news to Lesley Allerton of her father's death. The shock was a big one, but nothing compared to her surprise when she learned that he had been a criminal. Apparently he had religiously kept this from her. It was a long time before she would believe it. Not, in fact, until Superintendent Laker had substantiated what Jim told her.

Henry Allerton had, apparently, always led her to believe that he was a member of the secret service working for the Government. When he had fled the country after the killing of old John Brent he had given this reason for not taking Lesley with him, and the girl had never doubted the truth of his statement. She had received several letters during his absence abroad, and when for a time these ceased she was a little worried, but concluded that for some reason or other he was not in a position to write.

This was in truth the case, although she did not know it then, for his period of silence corresponded with the time that he was lying in hospital after the train accident.

When she had gone out to post the letter, on the evening of her disappearance, she had met Hillbury, who had informed her that he was a friend of her father's and had come to take her to him. It was necessary, he explained, that she should come at once as her father was leaving England again almost immediately. Suspecting nothing, the girl had gone with him. 'He had a car waiting,' she said, 'and when I got in I felt something prick my arm, and that's all I remember until I woke and found myself in that horrible padded room.' She shivered.

'What did they do with you when we came to search the house?' asked Jim, and learned for the first time of the well in the garden.

'I was terrified,' said Lesley, 'and then while I was hanging there I heard father's voice. He and another man cut me down and carried me along a passage to Lady's Manor. I shall never forget the first sight I had of father's face.' The tears gathered in her eyes, but she choked them back. 'It was the first I knew that anything had happened to him. He explained about the train accident and told me that the people who had kidnapped me were working for a foreign government. He said that he was in Little Siltley on Government business, and of course, I accepted his explanation. He was always so kind and gentle, I can scarcely believe, even now, that he was — he was — '

The tears which she had striven to keep in check streamed down her cheeks, and Phyllis Orde put her arm round the sobbing girl.

Jim left them sitting on the edge of Phil's bed in Mrs. Jillider's cottage with a heavy heart.

There was still much to be done. Hansard and the big black man, Nat, had been arrested when they burst out of the gates of Dead Trees in pursuit of little Arty Smith. The little crook, in his dash for freedom, had run full tilt into them in the hall, and Nat had struck at him with a knife, ripping his arm from shoulder to elbow, but he had succeeded in eluding them, and made his escape down the drive.

When Jim reached the little station house he found Laker taking down a statement from the real Patterson-Willis.

Queer Face and his two associates had taken possession, of Lady's Manor on the evening of the day on which the *Clarion* had rung the doctor up, suggesting the interview. He had only a day previously returned from abroad. His servant, the man the Superintendent had mentioned to Jim, had remained at Southampton to await the arrival of some books and specimens, which were being forwarded by another boat.

Patterson-Willis had been reading late that night when there had come a knock at the door, and, answering it, he had been set upon by the hulking Nat. A blow on the head rendered him unconscious, and when he came to his senses he found himself gagged and bound and a prisoner in an upper room.

'The one mistake the man made,' he said wryly, 'was when he put me in with Miss Orde, for I was able to release her and she did the same to me. We found the entrance to the passage connecting

286

Lady's Manor with Dead Trees, a stone trap in the scullery which they had left open, and we arrived at the house just as this fellow was preparing to make his escape.'

His statement was read over to him and signed, and when Laker had seen that Cusher and the man Clark, whom they had found neatly trussed up in the grounds, had been securely locked up, he went back with Jim to the Load of Hay to meet Freddy Kemp and Phyllis Orde for breakfast.

'What happened to the woman?' asked Jim suddenly. 'Mrs Hillbury, or Gleeson, or whatever her name was?'

'She made her escape in the general confusion,' answered Laker. 'I've already circulated her description and I don't suppose it will be long before she's pulled in.'

His words were prophetic, for the woman was arrested as she attempted to pass through the barrier at Victoria Station later that morning.

The case was over and Jim should have been satisfied, but he was not. Before his eyes floated the vision of a white face and tear-filled eyes; a face from which the joy of life had been struck, and he felt that it was his hand that had been responsible for destroying Lesley Allerton's greatest illusion, and bringing to her that look of mute anguish which he would see in his imagination for many weeks to come.

★   ★   ★

A year later Jim was steering a small car through the traffic of Fleet Street when a stentorious voice hailed him. Slowing, he pulled the little machine into the kerb. Freddy Kemp, larger and redder than ever, greeted him with a broad grin.

'Park that car somewhere,' he said, 'and come and have a drink.'

'Why, what's the matter?' asked Jim. 'Have you got a rise?'

'No,' answered the reporter, 'but I want to celebrate. Phil and I became officially engaged this morning.'

'Congratulations,' said Jim, and shook his friend by the hand. 'Where shall we go?'

'Press Club,' answered Freddy laconically, and ten minutes later they were discussing the contents of foaming tankards.

Jim had an appointment that afternoon on the other side of London. Driving through Hanover Square he saw crowds gathered at the entrance to the church. From the white ribbons on the waiting cars he guessed that a wedding was taking place and just as he passed he saw the bride and bridegroom come out of the arched door. The man he did not know, but the radiant, smiling girl he recognised at once. It was Lesley Allerton!

Bringing his little car to a halt he watched them get into a big saloon and drive off. Jim's heart was a little heavy as he shifted his gears and continued his journey. In different circumstances he might —

He gave a wry smile and jerked his thoughts from these unprofitable imaginings. Pulling his car up outside the grim exterior of a police station, he went in to interview the Inspector in charge concerning the doubtful alibi of a well-known ladder larcenist.

THE END

We do hope that you have enjoyed reading this large print book.

Did you know that all of our titles are available for purchase?

We publish a wide range of high quality large print books including:
Romances, Mysteries, Classics
General Fiction
Non Fiction and Westerns

Special interest titles available in large print are:
The Little Oxford Dictionary
Music Book, Song Book
Hymn Book, Service Book

Also available from us courtesy of Oxford University Press:
Young Readers' Dictionary
(large print edition)
Young Readers' Thesaurus
(large print edition)

For further information or a free brochure, please contact us at:
Ulverscroft Large Print Books Ltd.,
The Green, Bradgate Road, Anstey,
Leicester, LE7 7FU, England.
Tel: (00 44) **0116 236 4325**
Fax: (00 44) **0116 234 0205**